On Our Own

L.D. SILVER

FIRELIGHT TALES PUBLISHING

For Mom and Dad

Chapter 1

This is my fault.

Celie's torn and bloody body lies before me, her candy apple red nails glistening in the sunlight. She was so proud of those nails, so happy with them. Now they're chipped, and broken, and ruined.

"I'm so sorry, Celie," I whisper.

The bell rings at the front of the convenience store and I jump. I reach around her body and grab my bat, my heart pounding in my chest. I'm not ready for this again. I wish the world would just stop.

I peek around the open storage room door.

There's a little girl near the store's entrance. She's backlit by the bright Texas sun, and I strain to see signs of the virus. She's a dark, menacing shape, small in size but large in danger.

She steps forward and the motion is slow. Still unsure as to whether she's living or one of the corrupted dead, I raise the bat over my shoulder.

1

"Hello?" the girl calls. "Where are you?"

I rest my head against the door frame. She's alive. Not a threat at all, just a kid. Of course, this may be the same girl who almost got me killed, in which case, she *is* dangerous.

"Keep your voice down," I hiss and open the door the rest of the way. She comes toward me, her features becoming clear as she walks out of the sunlight.

The girl is no more than ten or eleven years old. She's thin, with shoulder-length wavy blonde hair and the pale skin of an indoor child. As far as I can discover, she has no bites, no scratches and her blue eyes have none of the tell-tale cracks of the virus. I don't see any blood on her, either. Her jeans and sneakers are dirty, while her white t-shirt is clean. Somebody's been taking very good care of her.

"Ohh," she says, stopping a foot away from the open door with her eyes focused on the room behind me.

She's looking at Celie. I block the door and cross an arm over my chest.

"What are you doing here?" I ask.

"Coming after you."

"You're the one who yelled, aren't you?"

On my way to the convenience store, a girl shouted at me from the second-story window of one of the stores bordering the street. Zombies poured into the area as soon as they heard her.

"Yes," she says.

"You almost got me killed!" I can't believe it. I was right. This nice, innocent-looking girl is the idiot who almost got my insides torn out like I was made of taffy.

"Is that a girl?" She rises on her toes and tries to look around me.

"Yeah. Don't get distracted. You. Almost. Got. Me. Killed." I don't touch her, but I emphasize my statement with a stabbing finger.

She frowns. "You made it here. And how else was I supposed to get your attention?"

The girl has me there.

"Don't do it again," I say, trying to sound as firm as my mom.

She points around me. "I saw her go by a few days ago. Never saw her come back, though."

My grip tightens on the bat. "Did you yell when you saw her, too?"

"No. I had somebody then."

So at least she hadn't gotten Celie killed. No, that had been my fault. If I'd come with her, maybe she would have lived. *And maybe we both would have been killed*, a little voice in my head says.

I realize I can't stand here glowering at her forever. "Why don't you see if you can find a blanket or something so we can cover her up?"

She nods and starts walking down the small aisles of the store. I turn back to Celie. All my anger with the little girl fades away.

Celie's brown hair is limp and flat against the floor, and her once-sparkling green eyes stare dully at the ceiling. My eyes dart over the places where the zombie ate her. I focus on the ceiling for a few moments and take some deep breaths. I sit down, shut her eyes, and take her hand in mine.

"I'm so sorry," I whisper. I try to focus on her face, where she still looks like herself, but it doesn't help. My eyes burn and I squeeze them closed.

She lived on my block, but she was older so we didn't hang out a lot. She'd always seemed happy and carefree; I'd never realized she was strong.

Celie saved my life, and then lost hers trying to get me food.

I squeeze my eyes tighter, fighting back the tears. I have to get her covered up and I have to say something. She deserves a proper burial. I can't do that, but I'll do the best I can.

"I couldn't find any blankets, but I grabbed some towels." The little girl drapes some white kitchen towels on my shoulder.

"Thanks," I reply. We cover Celie as best as we can. Then I clasp my hands together and bow my head.

"Thank you for saving my life, Celie. Thank you

for helping me. I think you're a good person." A tear tries to escape, and I look at the ceiling until I've gained my composure. "You're a good person and you deserve a good afterlife. If there's a Heaven, you should be there. Thank you for everything you did."

I turn away just as the tears fall. I swipe them from my face, take a deep breath, then count to ten and turn back. The little girl is looking down at the floor, her face sad.

"Thank you for the towels. I'm Delilah." My voice is shaky at the start, but by the time I get to my name, it's strong again. It's not my real name. That doesn't matter anymore, though, and I've always liked the name Delilah. I just like the sound of it, all fancy and clean and mysterious. Not at all like a dirty girl with a regular name.

"You're welcome. I'm Cassie," she says quietly.

"It's nice to meet you, Cassie," I say.

The storeroom is rather large, about the size of a kitchen with a breakfast nook included. Plastic shelves line one wall and are filled with cleaning supplies and various cans of food. Celie's body is behind the open door, so I sit in the corner as far away from her as I can.

"You mentioned somebody's been taking care of you."

The little girl nods and sits down across from me.

"What happened? Did they go to find others?"

Cassie's eyes flick towards Celie. "No."

"Oh," I say, realizing the fate of her caretaker. I gesture toward Celie. "She was my somebody."

"I thought so." We sit in silence for a few minutes and then she jumps up.

"Where are you going?" I ask.

"To get a soda."

"Just move slowly and be careful."

She rolls her eyes at me. "Please."

Once I'm alone again, I slip my necklace out from under my shirt and hold the pendant in my hand. It's a silver shamrock about the size of a quarter. The metal is beaten thin and the leaves are curved. This is the last thing my mom gave me before the world died.

I'd been watching the necklace for months, going to the store and holding it in my hand just like I am now. Each time I would think about taking some of my allowance and buying it, but every time I'd let it go and save the money for the spring formal instead. One day, my mom saw me. She said I'd been standing still for ten minutes, staring at the silver shamrock. When I told her why I put the necklace back, her brown eyes softened and she hugged me.

She surprised me with the necklace that night, saying it was for luck. Mom must have been right, because I'm still alive.

"Love you, Mom," I whisper. I kiss the shamrock

and slip it back under my shirt just as Cassie comes back into the room.

She opens a 7-Up and a candy bar and consumes a bit of both. "So," she says with her mouth full, "what are you going to do next?"

I grimace at seeing the messed-up chocolate she's showing me. Then I sigh. This morning I left the only hiding place I had, to get some food and find Celie. Now I've found her, but that's as far as my plans went.

"I don't know." I shrug. "Any ideas?"

She puts down her food and this is the first time I've seen her look serious. Of course, I've only known her for about five minutes, but she doesn't seem to be the solemn type.

"I need a new somebody."

"Me, too," I say and put my chin on my hand, looking at the floor. "If you were an adult in this mess, where would you go?"

"No, I meant – what about you? What about you being my new somebody?"

My eyes are drawn to Celie's body. Celie took care of me, and my mom watched over me before that. Both of them were stronger than I've ever been. And now, both of them are dead.

Even though I blamed Cassie for calling the zombies and almost getting me killed, the truth is I barely got here anyway. The convenience store is half a mile from the garage I started out in and they almost got me. And less than an hour ago, I was fighting for survival in this store with the same zombie that killed Celie, just a few inches from a painful death.

"No." I find myself shaking my head. "I can't do it."

"I saw the empty-head in the other room. You can do it!"

"What did you call them?"

"Empty-head. Their heads are empty until they see you."

I grin at her apt description. "Empty-head. I like that."

She pouts and crosses her arms. "You're not fooling me. You can do it. Take care of me, Delilah."

I look at Celie and a shiver runs through me. "I'm sorry, kid. I can't do it. I know what happens to somebodies."

The pout disappears and a calculated look forms on her face. I recognize that expression from my brother, right before he got me to do something I didn't want to do. Crap. She's cheery *and* a thinker.

"What if we were more of a team?"

"A team?"

"Yeah. It wouldn't be you taking care of me, or me taking care of you. It would be us, working together, helping each other. No somebody. A team.

Until we find an adult somebody," she says with a grin.

I think about it. On my own, how long will I really last? Having someone else along would help, especially if she doesn't think I'll do everything for her, like I thought Celie would do for me. And I won't be alone.

"Okay," I agree.

"Yeah!" She punches her arms into the air, smiling. I return the smile and shake my head at her enthusiasm. Something tells me she'll be trouble.

Cassie finishes her snack and leans against the wall. "So, what do we do now?"

"Stay here until an adult finds us?" I answer.

She looks at me like I'm an idiot.

"Yeah, I know, it's not going to happen. There is no roving band of adults looking for kids." I lean against the bookshelf that holds paper towels and toilet paper, feeling a rod poke into my back. "In the past when I had a bad day, there was one place I could always go that would cheer me up. And now there are even fewer limitations than there were before."

"Where?" she asks.

I smile. "The mall."

"The mall? It's the end of the world and you want to go to the mall?"

"Yeah. It always cheers me up. But I also want

some stuff. Practical things, like sleeping bags. Maybe weapons, too."

"Good idea, but it's like a mile from here or something, with ten thousand zombies in between us and there."

"Well, how did you get here?"

"I ran."

"Didn't they follow you?"

"Yeah, but they're slow." She rolls her eyes. "And stupid."

"Stupid?"

"Yeah. Before I came in the store, I left the door to the next shop wide open. Then I made sure they couldn't follow me in here even if they did figure things out."

"They went in the open door instead, didn't they?"

"Yep." Cassie smiles.

"There you go," I say.

"Can you run for a mile?"

"No." I shake my head. "But we'll use the same idea: run for a bit and throw them a decoy."

"Okay."

"Have you come across any fast ones?"

There's that look again, the one that says I'm an idiot.

"The empty-head in the store out there moved fast."

I bite a hangnail off my index finger. I don't tell her that I knew his name. I don't tell her that he was mean to me in life, and in death, and that he was the first zombie I ever killed.

"Anyways," I continue. "If he moved fast, then there's got to be others that can do the same. If one of those comes after you, scream and I'll help."

"Okay. When do you want to leave?"

"Now. Go to the bathroom and then we'll head out."

"In here?"

"Yeah. No use opening the door until we have to."

I find a bucket and grab some of the toilet paper behind me. I turn my back while she goes, then we switch positions. After that, I look for a weapon for her. I find a mop and unscrew the wood shaft from the head, but it's too big for her to swing. I jump on the shaft in an effort to break it in half, but fall on my butt instead, which sets Cassie into a fit of giggles.

I find a broom, but that's too big as well. Finally, I find one more thing that might work.

"Ewww – a plunger? I'm not touching the bottom of that thing."

I sigh, tear off the bottom and hand her just the stick. "If they get too close, stick it in their mouth when they try to bite you."

She nods, but holds it loosely, doubt radiating

from her. Looking at the flimsy weapon, I wonder if we're doing the right thing. Should we just stay here? There's plenty of food. But eventually that would run out, and then we'd be desperate, like I was this morning. Best to go now while we're still strong.

"Ready?" I ask.

She nods, gets a firm grip on her weapon, and grins at me. Then she lets out a whoop and runs to the door, pulling it open while I'm still standing there.

"Cassie!" I shout, and run after her.

Chapter 2

The sunlight dazes me. I'm afraid Cassie will get attacked before I can catch up.

"What?" She smacks her makeshift weapon against her leg.

"Wait for me," I say. She makes a noise in response. My vision returns and I see that, fortunately, this back area is deserted. Amazing – no zombies and no bodies. For a moment, life seems normal.

We're in the alley behind the convenience store. The dumpsters for all the stores are along this road so the garbage-people can drive in one long line and collect for the entire street. In front of us are more buildings, but to the left is another road going north toward the mall. I motion Cassie toward it with my finger on my lips.

This time, I take the lead. I begin with a walk, though we'd discussed running. I poke my head around the corner and see no zombies there, either.

I motion to Cassie and she comes to my side. She sees the alley is free of bodies and nods at me. Almost at the same time, we take off.

It's kind of exhilarating to be running free in broad daylight. It feels normal, like maybe I took something from a store and we're fleeing from the cops, with the only difference being Cassie's by my side instead of my friend Tonya. (Okay, it was only that once; I'm not a big thief or anything.)

I look back over my shoulder and Cassie's still there, although a bit behind and breathing hard. I slow down. She catches up and we walk for a few blocks until she's fine again.

"We're going to have to turn left up there." I nod in that direction. "Are you ready to run again?"

She holds her hand to her side, but she agrees.

"Okay." I grin and set off. I'm in that zone where you feel like you can run forever. Just a few more steps and I'll take off in flight.

I turn the corner and collide with a zombie, a male with dried blood caked on its hands and shirt. I scream without meaning to. The creature's open mouth heads for my neck while its hands grab me. Something thicker than blood oozes onto my skin. I scream again, pushing backwards with everything I have.

Something hits me from behind, sending me into

the zombie's arms, and both of us fall to the ground. The zombie thrashes, a weird honking sound coming from it. I can feel parts of its skin sliding off beneath me.

I can't move. I can't get my body to respond!

Finally, something clicks in me and I grab the zombie's arms. I get enough leverage to kick it in the stomach, getting it off me for a few precious seconds. I gain my feet and kick the empty-head again. I've lost my bat.

I hear a sound behind me and remember something had slammed into us. I turn around, my heart pounding in my chest. Cassie's getting to her feet behind me and I realize she was what sent me flying.

"Delilah!" she screams, pointing behind me.

The empty-head's getting up again. It's moving so slowly, but Cassie seems afraid. I kick it in the head, getting that blackish goo all over my tennis shoe. Then I see my bat and grab it. I have the forethought to say, "Don't look," and bash the zombie's head until it stops moving.

I lower the bat to my side and the world returns to its normal speed. I draw great gulps of air into my lungs, amazed at the bright colors around me. Then I realize something.

"They will have heard us scream."

Chapter 3

Cassie's eyes widen. We flee.

We get maybe a block away before the zombies reach the alleys. With slow, lumbering steps they fill the brick hallways. I dodge between them, running as fast as I can without losing Cassie. She starts to breathe hard again and I know I have to do something.

I race ahead a bit and stop. I swing the bat, going from one zombie to the next until I clear a small circle. Then I smash the window of a door nearby, reach through and open the door. Cassie runs up as I bang the bat against a dumpster, making as much noise as I can. She joins in with her plunger handle.

We walk away and stand against the brick wall. I pant like a dog, trying to catch my breath, wondering if they'll fall for it. The first empty-head is an overweight woman with limp blonde hair. Her cracked eyes look like marbles that were slammed into concrete. She shuffles through the open door without noticing us.

I can't believe it. Cassie's right; they can be fooled. I watch with relief as one by one the zombies turn and follow each other into the dark building, their empty eyes failing to scan the area and spot us.

"You're a genius," I whisper to Cassie. She grins, and we run again.

Forty minutes later, we're on a small grassy hill above the mall parking lot. We're on the back side where there's only a Dillard's and a Sears. The brown brick of the mall looks a bit outdated, but the inside is still chock full of stores.

"I can't believe the distraction worked."

"Told ya." Cassie smiles. "They're not very bright."

"Thank God for that."

I stretch out onto my stomach and consider the situation below us. Apparently, we aren't the only ones to think of going to the mall. There are still cars in the parking lot. Bodies that aren't going to get up again litter the lot and bodies that won't stay down walk among them.

As we watch, a zombie male in a plaid shirt and blue jeans stumbles over one of the bodies. He falls to his hands and knees. He sniffs the air and turns towards the body, then grabs an arm and pulls. The arm comes off easily, fluids dripping wetly to the ground.

"Ewww," says Cassie.

He tears into it, eyes closed as if he's eating the finest steak ever. Then suddenly he drops the arm and throws up. He sniffs the vomit, licks it, and starts eating it. He finishes the vomit and then picks up the arm again, eats, and throws up.

"Really stupid," Cassie adds. I watch him for a while, unable to look away in spite of myself before Cassie asks, "Why is he throwing up?"

"I don't know," I answer. "Maybe it's gone bad?" I don't know how the dead would spoil for something that liked eating them, but what the hey? Then I realize I've always seen the zombies eating live people. Maybe they need their meat really fresh. Oh, I can't believe I just thought that.

One of the fast ones comes running toward the flannel zombie.

I nudge Cassie. "See, some of them are faster."

"That's not fair," she says.

"What's he doing?"

The fast zombie moans, hands outstretched as it crashes into the other one. The fast one pushes Flannel away from the body and takes a big bite out of the corpse's neck. It chews a couple of times then spits out the pieces. I swear it looks at Flannel in disgust. Then the empty-head just wanders away.

"Fuck, the fast ones are smarter, too," I say.

"You said the F-word," Cassie says with awe in her voice.

"Say it all the time." I shrug. I'm lying of course. I've only cursed once before, but it seems really appropriate now.

"So, how are we going to get in?" Cassie asks.

"Through there." I point to Dillard's.

"Won't they just follow us in?"

"It's why I picked that store. See that last part of glass next to the door, the small part that's closed in?" On either side of the doors the glass is partitioned, separated by metal into three rectangles. "We'll break into the small part and crawl in. Then we'll block the hole."

"Cool. Are we just going to run through all of them?"

I look at the scene below. There are easily a hundred zombies down there, and that's just the area directly in front of us. Getting through them will be okay, but I wonder how many the sound of breaking glass will bring. I don't want to use another door to a store nearby as a distraction because that will just get them in the mall, which I want to avoid.

Before I met Cassie, I survived by pure luck, like coming across the unlocked door at the convenience store. But she's given me a tool that's worked and I want to use it here. I think a moment more and then tell Cassie my plan.

Chapter 4

Twenty minutes later, we're in place. Cassie stands in front of the partitioned glass at the Dillard's entrance, and I'm about a block and a half away next to an abandoned car. I nod at Cassie and she returns the gesture.

I slam my bat against the car's window, shouting at the same time. The glass breaks and I run to the next car. I shatter that car's back window and run on to the next one while yelling. The idea is to make as much noise as possible and hopefully confuse the zombies about where I'm standing. Yes, it's really stupid and I can't believe I'm doing this, but it's this or go back to the convenience store and hide.

"It won't break! It won't break!" Cassie shouts. I glance over my shoulder and see the plunger handle is useless against the glass storefront.

The zombies that were standing around before are now heading toward me. I can already see a few coming around the corner of the mall, as well. Thanks to the various cars I'm smashing they're scattered, but there are still a lot of them. A few heads turn to look at Cassie and then some zombies shuffle her way.

"Watch out!" I shout. I need to help her, but how? I look around and get an idea. Keeping my eyes on the dead, I open my mouth and moan; a loud, long moan as close to theirs as I can get. I do it again. Zombie heads turn one after the other, following the sound and creating a neat little wave pattern. I cry again, louder. They come toward me.

"Cassie," I hiss in a low tone, and throw the bat at her. I continue to moan as she bashes the glass in. I make the next one louder, throwing my head back and drawing the zombies to me.

"Delilah!" Cassie is on her hands and knees in the store, poking her head out of the glass opening. I moan a few more times while running around a car. Then I grab an arm that's disconnected from a nearby body. Grimacing in disgust, I run straight toward the zombies near the door. Right before I reach them, I cry again and throw the arm into the middle of the group. They turn as one to grab it.

I slam to the ground. Cassie's kicked the broken glass out of the way, so I'm able to crawl quickly into the store. The zombies are still fighting over the arm and don't notice.

Cassie's staring at me, her mouth wide open. "That was freaky! You sounded just like them!"

I grin and crawl further into the store. Then I jump to my feet, run to a nearby display, and push a mannequin over. I take the box it was standing on and put it in front of the hole we made.

"There. Good as new," I say. Then I realize the bat is on the other side of the glass. "Crap."

"What?" Cassie asks. I just point at it. Our strongest weapon is out of reach. A few of the zombies give up on getting the arm.

"Should we go get it?"

I slowly shake my head, watching the dead. Will they come to the glass?

"No, we leave it there." I put an arm against her chest and start backing up very slowly. A zombie head pops up and looks through the glass, attracted by the movement.

"Crap, crap, crap," I mutter under my breath. We keep retreating even as the thing advances. It's a male with short blonde hair and cracked blue eyes. Dried blood covers a white dress shirt and flows over gray pants and brown dress shoes.

It hits the door and stops. I hold my breath as it clinks against the glass. I watch the box, hoping it won't move. The zombie bumps into the glass again, and this time I can see what's causing the 'clinking' noise: it's still wearing a pocket watch on a chain that's swinging free. Could that break the glass? How much force would be necessary? Surely it won't be enough for the zombie to realize it might be able to break more glass and come in.

Then another empty-head hits the male from behind. The Watch zombie turns to the second one, and they do this weird bumper car thing until they both seem confused and bump each other into different directions. I let out my breath.

"Let's go," I say.

Chapter 5

Cassie and I walk into a memory of our old lives. I'm used to this place being brightly lit, with boring old-people music playing in the background and the floors shining. I remember the last time I was here. I was with my mom and I dragged her through every good store in this mall, asking for everything along the way. At the end, we'd stopped and had warm cinnamon rolls.

Now, as I walk through the store, there is no music. The floors are dull. And the further we go into the store, the darker it gets. As the light fades, each mannequin becomes a zombie, waiting in the darkness for me to get close enough to eat.

"Delilah." Cassie grabs my arm and stops. I jump and let out a little squeak.

We're at the edge of the light. I imagine that, when things first went downhill, the store was lit for a while by emergency lights over the doors, but those are no longer working.

I reach into my pocket and pull out a lighter I'd grabbed at the convenience store. I push down on the little silver wheel and a flame springs to life. I hold it in front of us and try not to burn my hand.

"Okay?"

She nods. "But let's find some flashlights."

"There won't be any in here."

Unfortunately, Dillard's doesn't carry flashlights. At least, all I remember of the store is clothing, shoes and makeup. Oh, and purses.

"I know. Just soon, okay."

"Okay."

I walk down the dark, quiet aisles with Cassie beside me. It's creepy, really. I keep getting small flashes of what it was like before. And I keep expecting a zombie to come moaning out of the dark, hands stretching in front of it.

We finally hit the clothing area and I have an idea. I push a mannequin to the floor then kick until I get both of the arms off. *What is it with me and arms today?* Anyway, I grab a shirt off a nearby rack, wrap it around the mannequin's hand and light it on fire.

"Careful." I give the torch to Cassie. She looks at me like I'm off my rocker, but she takes it. I grab the other arm and create one for myself.

Now that we both have torches, the area is lit a bit more. I can see the entire aisle and some of the items around us. We walk past the shoes (without stopping!) and get close to the front. I grab some more shirts from the racks and hand a few to Cassie so we can swap them out as they burn.

I reach the front of the store and the black open maw of the mall. In my mind, I can still hear a bit of the music. God, if I could only have that back: music playing, girls walking around in pairs giggling, little kids eating ice cream and letting it fall on the floor. But that's not going to happen.

"Delilah, what if some of the zombies get through?" She brings me back to the present.

"Good point," I respond.

I notice the silver gate at the edge of the department store's opening. I hand Cassie my torch and grab the edge. I pull once and it doesn't move, so I brace my feet and pull harder. The gate comes free and Cassie giggles. I glare at her and pull it across. I shut it, but there's no way I can lock it. It will have to do.

I take my light back from Cassie. It's almost burnt out, so I go ahead and blow it out, tearing off what's left and tossing it to the floor. I wrap another shirt, light it on fire, and do the same for Cassie.

"We need to find flashlights fast."

I nod. "We're not that far from the sporting goods store."

"'Kay."

The mall is darker than the world at night. In my head, I can see zombies coming out of every little turn. They'll wait, of course, until it's too late for us to turn back and then ambush us.

I shake my head and take a deep breath. I remind myself that it was my idea to come here and that it was a good one. There are things we need. We have to do this.

Then I notice Cassie is skipping ahead of me into the darkness, without a care in the world.

Maybe she's stupid. No, I know that's not it. Shaking my head, I hustle to catch up with her.

The hallway of the mall is wide enough to fit two cars going each way. The floor is left over from the eighties and is a light brown tile. We pass a Bath and Body Works – smelly and closed for good – as well as a Gap. And a Gap Kids.

We turn right when we reach the point where the hallway meets the main thoroughfare of the mall. I keep expecting zombies to jump out of nowhere, but so far there's nothing. Did no one go shopping right before the world ended?

After this stretch, there will be a wide open space used for fashion shows and holiday events, like Santa Claus, and then the sporting goods store will be at the end of the hallway after that.

We aren't too far from the wide open space when the stench reaches us.

Cassie coughs and puts her hand over her nose. "What's that?"

I gag. "Shhhhh."

I guide Cassie away from the middle of the mall over to the edge. I don't like being so close to the alcoves some of the store openings have, but I think I know what's up ahead. My heart's pounding so loud I'm sure Cassie can hear it.

We reach the wide open space and I stop. The area's basically a huge circle in the middle of two intersecting hallways. I raise my torch high and confirm my suspicions.

Bodies are scattered in the circle. Some of them hold hands. Some of them lay alone. Some of them are wrapped around each other.

Cassie gasps. I forgot to hide it from her. I push her back against the store behind me.

"What happened?" she breathes.

"You hadn't heard?"

Cassie shakes her head, her eyes wide. It reminds me of how young she is. Somebody must have protected her.

"They're called Suicide Groups. The idea was that you couldn't come back as a zombie if your head was cut off. So, people formed groups and made pacts. One person would cut off everyone's head." My eyes drift from paper cups still clutched in lifeless hands to headless bodies.

"And what happens to that one person?"

"If the cops didn't get there first, that person was supposed to blow their head off with a gun." I scan the group, moving my eyes quickly to a man slumped in a chair like an exhausted king of the dead. His hand still grips a handgun, and his head is still attached, although I glance away quickly from the bloody mess it's become.

"Wow," Cassie says.

I realize she's moved to stand beside me and isn't screaming or acting hysterical. "You're not afraid, are you?"

Cassie looks at me like I'm an idiot and rolls her eyes. "Really?"

And I get her point. Yes, she's had to dodge dead people all day, the most being in the parking lot. These people creep me out because their heads are detached. Ewww. It's not right. But when it comes down to it, when the dead can walk and eat you alive, how scary is a non-walking group of dead people anyway?

Chapter 6

I find Cassie's hand and drag us both away. We find the sporting goods store without incident and stock up on weapons, flashlights and two sleeping bags. Then, finally, we go to where I'd planned on going the whole time.

Belinda's is a superstore, kind of like a Super Target joined with a Dillard's, only without any groceries. In the old days – yes, I'm so old... no, I mean before the world died – Belinda's was brightly lit. Now it's dark but with a wide sweep of my large flashlight, I can see glimpses of its past shine. The aisles are wide and the white floors still gleam. Small white pedestals, similar to the columns of a Roman building, mark each intersection.

"Let's sweep through the store first and look for zombies." I turn left.

"Okay," Cassie agrees.

We walk past the DVD and game section, all of

the boxes still neatly placed on black bookshelves. The movie section is carpeted, and if you look closely you can see fake popcorn printed on it, just like the corn was spilled all over the floor. I lead Cassie past the electronics section where large TVs with blank, black screens stare into the store like unmoving eyes.

I start moving my flashlight around, raising on tiptoe every few steps as Cassie giggles at my antics. Really, it's serious – I'm trying to find zombies – but I guess it looks kind of funny.

I grab hold of her arm to keep her near me when we pass the toys.

"Sweep first," I remind her. She almost has to do the same thing with me when we pass the shoes, but I'm good and walk past.

The silence of the store is uncanny. I want to sing, dance, anything to make noise, fill up this empty store with remembrances of how it used to make me feel. I glance sideways at Cassie, but I just can't do it. What if she thinks I'm weird?

I rush us through the clothing section. I know that's bad – zombies could very well be hiding in here – but it's so big and I just want to shop. I have Cassie crawl on the floor and I walk on tiptoe, and we move like that through the tight areas between silver racks full of clothes. Oh my God, there won't be a new season of clothes, will there?

Finally, we're back at the front again. I sigh; no zombies in sight.

I smile. "Okay, go shopping, girl. You can stay with me or have at it."

"Nice!" She smiles back and runs toward the toys.

"Meet up at shoes in about an hour!" I shout after her and she waves at me. I watch her run into the darkness, hoping our sweep was thorough enough.

Chapter 7

I head back to the clothing section. I take my time, slowly circling through the jeans and tops, looking for things that might be interesting. This area is carpeted as well, and even in the old days the recessed lighting was so dim as to be almost worthless. I guess they didn't want you to realize how horrible some of the clothes were. Really, do girls over five need big bows on their shirts?

My circling of the racks is a delay. I know they still have it. I know because I'd been watching it since before everything went south. I'd seen it on the last real day of normality.

Slowly, I go around the corner and there it is: a blue formal with spaghetti straps and a skirt length which hits me just above the knee. The blue is shimmery, a bit metallic, and the texture of the fabric is slippery on the outside and soft on the inside.

I'd been saving money to buy it for two months

before everything went to hell. The time for the spring formal came and went without anyone caring—except for me, of course. Yes, when the world is ending, of course you still hold a dance! When else?

I reach out a hand and touch the dress, enjoying the feel of the cloth. I smile and then collect the rest of the outfit. I float back to the dressing rooms, where they have a walk-on platform surrounded by glass that's meant for girls to try on formals while their moms watch. My mom is nowhere nearby, but I have the dress.

I change in one of the dressing rooms and go to the platform. I place flashlights all along the bottom so it looks like I'm on stage at a fashion show before I step up and look at my reflection in the mirrors.

The dress sparkles from the lights, the color shifting between a deep metallic blue and a regular blue. I'm wearing a pair of shiny black, patent-leather Mary Janes with a heel which isn't too thick and isn't too skinny. I have on a pair of cream-colored pantyhose that matches a string of creamy pearls I found in the jewelry section.

I'd planned on wearing my hair up for the dance, but now I've just brushed it out. My dark brown hair drapes over my shoulders, looking gorgeous next to the blue of the dress even though my hair isn't as naturally wavy as my mom's. My skin is as pale as ever, and the dress emphasizes the blue-green of my eyes.

Nothing can hide my big nose, though.

I sigh and put my hands on my waist. I cock one hip out, put my head down, and peer up through my hair, just like I saw on a modeling show. Then I shift positions, angling one leg neatly in front of me. I raise my head and extend my hand, smiling.

"I'd love to dance with you, Tommy."

"Who's Tommy?"

I yelp. The little demon has snuck up without me seeing her in the mirrors. I turn neatly on one heel (like I practiced!) to find Cassie grinning at me. She's covered in fake tattoos, some of the ones on her arm overlapping each other.

"What happened to you?"

"Like 'em?" She extends one arm. She has dragons, hearts and tribals wrapped around each other and there's a giant butterfly on her cheek. "I wasn't allowed to have them."

"Boy, I can tell." I can't help smiling, but I manage not to laugh.

She giggles. "So, who's Tommy?"

I turn back to the mirror and see the blush rising on my face. "Just a guy from school." I play with my skirt a little.

"Ahhh." She steps up on the dais and lightly touches my dress. "Nice dress."

"You think?"

"Yeah. You can look real nice when you're not covered in black."

I roll my eyes. "Thanks. Let's go get dinner."

After changing, I let her go ahead of me so she can't see when I slip a wad of cash onto one of the cash registers on the way out. Hey, I worked hard and saved up a long time for that dress. It's the point of the thing.

Belinda's doesn't have a restaurant, so we go to the mall's food court. I'm a little anxious about going to another huge gathering place, but fortunately there hasn't been another mass suicide there. I slide over the Subway counter. *God, this is so cool. I never would have been able to do something like this in the old days.* The meat's pretty much gone bad, but I grab some bread and chips.

We eat on the floor of the court, amongst a forest of tables and chairs. Geez, if there weren't dead bodies around, I would totally run willy-nilly through this mall. Of course, that would just confirm to Cassie that I'm crazy. Then again, it's hard to take her seriously when she has a giant green butterfly on her cheek.

After dinner, we head back to Belinda's. I figure it's as good a place as any to spend the night. I lead the way past employee lockers, and then a break room complete with a microwave and sink. The white hallway is decorated with those ridiculous teamwork posters full of cliffs and mountains. At the end of the hall is a set of stairs with a steel door at the top. Thinking why not, I go up the stairs with Cassie right behind me.

I pause at the top with my hand hovering over the door handle and look at Cassie. She just shrugs, so I yank on it and what do you know, it's unlocked.

I expect a zombie to jump at me right away but it doesn't happen. Instead, I walk into the room and scan the darkness with my flashlight. That's when I hear the moan. I swing my light in that direction and reveal a zombie running at me full-tilt with its mouth wide open and hands outstretched. I scream and drop the flashlight.

Chapter 8

The zombie grabs my arms and plows into me with such force we crash to the floor. I can't see its mouth. Oh, God, I can't see its mouth! It's going to get me!

I squirm, trying to keep away from it while I'm reaching for the knife at my belt. It's got to be close. *Oh, God, come on!*

Then I hear a whack and the weight of the zombie slips away. I hear two more thunks and then bright light shines in my eyes.

"I can't see!" I hold a hand in front of me.

"Sorry." Cassie points the flashlight in a different direction. She's standing to my left with a bat in her other hand. The empty-head's on the floor just in front of my feet, its arms wide and curled on its side. It's wearing a red checkered flannel shirt and khakis. Wet, jet-black hair is plastered to the side of its head and black eyes are riddled with the cracks of the virus. As I watch, its head shifts.

"You need to kill it," she says.

I get up slowly, feeling like I have something sharp in my blood, like acid or poison. I hate this feeling. Cassie shines the light on the zombie. Its eyes track us, and then it moans while one hand grabs the air in front of it. In a few seconds, it will get up again.

I hold out my hand and Cassie gives me her bat. I get a good grip, widen my stance, and thwack the zombie until my arms hurt and there is no spark in its eyes anymore.

I drop the bat and fall to my knees, gasping for air.

"Why didn't you use the gun?" Cassie asks. She's talking about the handgun I'd picked up at the sporting goods store. It's still firmly in the black holster at my side.

"I've never shot one before. What if I missed and hit you?" I say that because it sounds reasonable, but in reality, when everything was happening I forgot I had it. Why did I remember the knife but not the gun?

She nods, her eyes on the zombie. Then she looks at me and I see very little of a kid in those eyes. "Can I have a gun now?"

"Can you shoot?"

"No. But neither can you. And –" She motions to the zombie. "What if you're not here?"

She has a point. She doesn't have the strength to kill a zombie with a bat. In this case, it would have gotten her.

"You're right. We'll get you one tomorrow. Now, let's clean up this mess."

We drag the zombie down to the employee break room, and the whole process is disgusting. The skin keeps sliding away under my fingers, dipping them into rotting slime which shouldn't ever be touched.

"Ugh," Cassie says as she drops her half. "Oooohhhh." She turns in little circles, waving her hands and doing a heebie-jeebies dance.

"C'mon, there still might be some water in the faucet." We wash our hands in the water, scrubbing without soap in an effort to wash off the slimy feeling. No such luck.

I lead the way back up to the steel door and step inside, swinging my flashlight over the entire room, expecting another empty-head to jump out. I slowly let out my breath as the room appears to be truly zombie-free. There's a noise in the room I hadn't noticed before, but frankly I was distracted last time.

"Hey, what's this?" Cassie points to a weird little black and red box with wheels.

"I think it might be a generator." I return to the door, using the flashlight to find and flip the room's switch. The room floods with bright white light. I blink, fighting the urge to hold out my arms and wash myself in it. Blessed electricity. It's been ages.

Cassie whoops, jumping up and down.

"Hey, I'll be right back," she says and runs out the door.

"Be careful!" I call out after her.

I just stand there for a few minutes, drinking in a world filled with something other than darkness or sunlight. If I stand just right, I can look out the stairwell and pretend everything's just fine. Maybe I've gotten nabbed for shoplifting – or better yet, met a cute security guard – and in a few minutes I will go back down and continue shopping.

The noise from the generator is beginning to get on my nerves. It sounds like a lawnmower. I sigh and wheel it out on the stairwell. It barely fits. Cassie's going to have to squeeze by it, but at least the door will act as an extra barrier to the noise during the night.

I turn and look at the room. The walls are painted that dull gray security color. A bank of monitors is on the far side, as well as a chair and desk with a set of controls. Squeezed on the end of the desk are a black microwave and a small white refrigerator. Then there's a large brown bookcase full of canned food and microwaveable dinners.

To the left of me is a small bed with the covers thrown back, like the owner has just gotten up to go to the bathroom. At the end of the bed is an unzipped black suitcase, filled with underwear, shirts and jeans. My throat seizes up, looking at the suitcase. Someone's prepared this room for a long stay.

Chapter 9

I wonder who stocked this room so well. Was it the zombie? Had he locked himself in here and then turned? Or did it attack him and he'd been able to trap it in here before wandering off himself?

I'm thinking about turning the monitors on when Cassie bounces back into the room.

"Hey," she says. She's shining with happiness and holds something small and black in her hand.

"What's that?"

She opens her hand, revealing a PlayStation Portable, or PSP for short. I can't help but smile. "Something else you were forbidden?"

"No." She shakes her head. "I was going to get one if my final grades were good enough."

"Were they?" I ask.

She rolls her eyes.

"Plug it in and get it charging."

"I can't play it right away?"

"No, it's got to charge for a while."

"Oh." The shine leaves her, shrinking down like a balloon when the air's being let out.

"Let's stay long enough to make sure you can play for a while."

She grins at me. "Thanks!"

I close the door, making sure to keep the generator going, and lock it. When I turn around, Cassie has her head in the fridge.

"We should have had dinner here," she states. "Ooh, Delilah, ice cream!"

"Really?" I peer around her shoulder.

"Yeah." She grabs an orange sherbet push-up and wisely gets out of my way.

"Oh, you're right." The freezer portion of the refrigerator has push-ups, ice cream sandwiches and popsicles. I really like whoever stocked this room.

I grab a sandwich and sit on the floor, and then think of something. I reach into my pocket and pull out my best Christmas gift ever: my own cell phone, chock full of my favorite music. I turn it on because now it doesn't matter if the battery runs low; I'll just juice it up tomorrow before we leave. I set the music to play randomly.

"Ahhh," I say as Fergie's voice fills the room. Cassie laughs. I peel back the paper on my sandwich and slowly lick the sides, savoring the cold vanilla. I close my eyes, eating the vanilla and chocolate so slowly that bits of vanilla ice cream run down my hand. I open my eyes and lick my hand, enjoying every last drop.

Then I notice Cassie staring at me.

"What?" I ask.

She giggles. "You're acting like a cat."

A part of me freezes up, wondering if she'll make fun of me now, but I try to act all cool anyway. I smile and shrug. "It's good."

"Let's dance." She puts her hand out as if to lift me up. "No, not with your sticky hand. Gross."

I take her hand, but I do most of the lifting. I turn the music up and we dance.

Cassie dances like she doesn't care that I'm here. She whoops and whirls through the room, just totally enjoying herself. Me, I can dance a bit, but I don't act like that.

"You're a good dancer," I tell her.

Cassie actually blushes a bit.

"Thanks," she says. "I like it. Like you like running."

I think about it, swinging my arms in time to the music, and I realize she's right. When I run, it feels so good that I don't consider anyone else. Then I think about it. *Oh, no, were people making fun of me while I ran? Did I look funny?*

Then a good part comes on and I dance crazy with Cassie, just enjoying the sound of the music.

Eventually we tire out and decide to go to sleep. Neither of us wants to take the empty bed, so we spread out sleeping bags on the floor. I keep one very dim light on, not because I need it, but because it's so nice to have.

I wait until Cassie falls asleep then quietly reach into my bag. I picked up something special this afternoon when we were apart. Carefully I watch her as I slip it into my sleeping bag, but thankfully she doesn't stir. It would be really embarrassing for a little kid like Cassie to find out I'm sleeping with a teddy bear. But it's so nice and soft, brown all over with black button eyes, and its open arms hug me. I hug it back and hunker down into my sleeping bag, closing my eyes. Eventually I drift off to sleep.

I wake up screaming.

Chapter 10

In the dream, I'm fighting a zombie. Its mouth, stinking of rotted flesh, eaten and owned, is within one snap of my body. At first, I see the last zombie I killed, then the one before that, each face slowly morphing until I see my first: Jimmy. He grins, gripping me tightly, saying over and over, "Dork for dinner, ha ha ha. Dork for dinner."

I shrink away and feel the flesh holding me slip and slide into a different texture. The zombie's face is now my mother's. Part of her is already rotting, green slime oozing from a cut on her face, her hair messed up to an extent that would have bothered her when she was alive.

She pulls back, looking at me.

"Baby girl," she says while she stares at me like I'm something she owns. I shiver as she digs her rotting fingers into my shoulder. "Come home, baby girl," she continues, and leans in for a bite.

That's when I scream.

I wake up in the dark, panting. Cassie's eyes are wide in the dim light, watching me.

"I had a nightmare," I explain.

"Really." Cassie rolls over and is back to sleep in minutes.

I lie in the dark and try to get my heart to calm down. Before I fall asleep again, the last thought I have is that I need to get out of here.

#

"But I don't understand why you want to leave." Cassie munches on a scrambled egg sandwich. "We're in a great spot. We're safe, we have food, and –" she grins, "we have electricity."

"You're right. It's a good place. For a while. And then we'll have to leave again. Go out and get supplies. How long do you want to live in a metal box?"

"It's not safe anywhere." She shrugs.

"I want out of here, Cassie. I want to go someplace where I have no memories." That serious look hits her face again as she bites into her sandwich.

"Like where?"

I grab a couple of folded brochures from my backpack and smooth them out. The creases in them are so old the paper nearly tears in half. "Colorado. The Rocky Mountains."

"Ever been there?" she asks.

"Yes." A long time ago, before my family fell apart, the four of us took a trip up there in the summer. We drove through the mountains and some of the communities, with my Dad talking about buying a house. It was the last time I remembered us laughing together, talking and having a really good time.

"It's really beautiful up there. Look." I show her the skiing brochure. "There are isolated communities and cabins. I think we could find a safe area."

"What about finding adults, a somebody?" Cassie frowns.

"If we find anyone on the way, we can stop. If we don't, we can build a base of operations and look for adults."

"We could build a base here."

"That's true, we could. But I don't want to walk around this mall waiting for my mom to pop out around the corner. I'm not just talking about ghosts, Cassie. What if we come across someone you knew, one of your friends, and they're a zombie? What if we have to kill that person to survive?"

She blanches. "Okay," she agrees in a small voice.

I feel like a jerk. My mom would have rubbed her arm, or hugged her and told her it would be okay, but my arms feel locked to my side.

Cassie pulls her knees up to her chest and then reaches around them to turn the brochures over. She's silent for a while, biting her lip. Then her face smoothes over and she sighs.

"Okay, let's do it." She looks at me and smiles. It's at that point I realize I've talked her into risking her life. If she dies doing this, it will be my fault.

Chapter 11

We get supplies for our trip, and then we go through and weed things out so we can actually go somewhere. We get Cassie a gun, and even though I have one, too, I just feel squirrelly inside about getting a gun for a kid. This isn't right; she should be popping bubble gum and playing with Barbies, not handling a weapon. It looks big and heavy in her hand, and I don't like the look in her eyes when she holds it.

I push the feelings down and finish packing. We're going with bikes for now because I've only kind of driven once, and I can't imagine trying to drive out of town anyway. Everything's got to be blocked, right? But bikes can make it through almost anywhere. As we head out, I take one last look at the secured room. Am I wrong to leave? I guess I'll know shortly. At the last minute, I grab another ice cream sandwich — you know, for the road and all.

I figure our best bet to get out of here is to use one of the loading docks. Before we broke in, I noticed that one of the stores had a recessed area with a dock and a ramp. With luck, there isn't anything there to attract the zombies and the area will be clear. Just in case, though, I sidetrack to a Hickory Farms so I can set up a little decoy before Cassie and I meet at the dock.

"What on Earth is that?" she asks.

I've taken a little boy mannequin and taped it to a skateboard. For good measure, I cover it in that cheese that spreads like butter, and I tape summer sausage to the front and back. It looks really weird – I admit that – but hopefully it will be a good distraction.

"That's not going to work." Cassie laughs.

"It might." I open the door and shut it immediately. "Crap."

"Zombie?" Cassie asks with wide eyes.

"Two." My heart's pounding in my chest. I almost screamed when I saw them. Just one night without their moans as my lullaby and it's like I've never seen one before.

"Delilah?"

"Yeah, I know." I throw open the door and they loom a few feet away. There's a male in jeans and a red t-shirt near the end of the concrete dock and a female in a yellow summer dress close to him. The male moans as soon as he sees us, the sound warping because of a giant tear in the side of his face. The female shuffles closer, one leg covered in dried blood, the other mottled and gray.

I shove my decoy as hard as I can and it hurtles down the ramp as the zombies' heads snap to attention, following the motion. A long moment passes and then they go after the mannequin.

I take a couple of deep breaths and my heart calms down. I can do this. I swing my leg over the bike, a red racing one with three speeds.

"Stay close," I whisper to Cassie. She nods, then I fly down the ramp.

I hit the bottom and turn right. The two zombies from earlier are a block away. The decoy's fallen over and they're almost on top of it. There's a cluster of zombies about two blocks away that raise their heads in unison as I look at them. God, that's really spooky.

I zoom around a body that's been kind enough to stay dead and lying down. I think we can make it past the group of empty-heads without a problem because they haven't moved yet. There's another cluster to the northeast, but they haven't seen me yet.

"Delilah!" Cassie's scream is sharp, loud and bound to attract every walking dead person in the area.

I cut my bike in a tight circle and stop. She's fallen

and the bike's on its side, tripped up by the body I dodged. And behind her is a band of fast-moving zombies.

Chapter 12

"Get up!" I scream. I pedal as fast as I can, angling away from her but going in that direction. I reach into my backpack and pull out an unwrapped tube of summer sausage.

"Hey! Hey!" I yell and wave it like a meaty flag. The front leader of the band, a male with long, black skater-boy hair, whips his head toward me. He sees the sausage and moans. The others respond in concert as the entire band turns my way. I throw the meaty treat away from me and pull out another. Some of them immediately head for the one that's already landed but Black Hair stays on me. I glance to my side and see that Cassie's up and pedaling away.

"Hey! Skater!" I wave the second sausage and head toward the cluster. At the last moment, I turn my bike and throw the sausage right in the middle of them. If I'd managed this kind of coordination in school, I might have actually done well in sports. Who knew fear could make your body move this way?

I race after Cassie. Then I hear the sound of slapping feet and look over my shoulder. The rest of the zombies are fighting over the meat, but Black Hair's still after me. I'm out of sausage and he doesn't seem to want it anyway. I rise up in my seat and pedal hard. My fingers slide on the handlebars, wet from sweat. *Think, think, think.*

"Delilah, do the cheese!"

Do the cheese? What the heck is she talking about? Then I remember the Easy Cheese; that spreadable cheese from my decoy is still in my backpack. I sit up and ride without my hands on the handlebars. I'll have to be quick or I'll run into bodies. I unzip my pack and reach back but I can't feel it. *Where is it?*

There! I pull it out and flip off the cap just as I hit a patch of bodies. I put a hand on one of the bars and wobble past the clump of them. I can hear Black Hair's feet, a second drum to accompany the pounding in my chest. I turn my upper body and spray cheese right into his face.

He keeps running with outstretched hands. Then he trips on a body and falls to the ground. I'm not sure if he did that because of the cheese or because he was just so focused on getting me, but I don't care either way.

"Woo-hoo!" Cassie yells. I grin and pedal full-force until I catch up with her.

"There's an exit up ahead. When we get there, take a left." I point and she nods. I glance over my shoulder. Black Hair has gotten up and is headed our way again.

"Okay, Cassie, whatever happens, just pedal hard and head for the exit. If we get separated, meet me one block past when you turn left."

"Okay," she agrees, but she looks worried. Fortunately, Black Hair isn't able to run yet. Ahead of us is a group of the slow-moving zombies. They aren't shoulder to shoulder, and they haven't noticed that we're headed their way yet.

"Go through those zombies," I order.

"What?" she screeches.

"Just do it. As fast as you can."

Cassie looks at me weird, but she does it, zooming ahead of me. She has wonderful control of the bike, leaning in and curving with it to get around the zombies. I take a deep breath and follow her in.

How can I describe this? I'm racing through a forest of zombies. There are adults, taller than me, bigger than me, moving slowly. There's a guy to my right, in a red plaid t-shirt and jeans, missing an eye and covered in blood. If he touches me, if he grabs me and pulls me off the bike, I'm dead.

This is crazy.

Some of them react after Cassie goes through, slowly turning and holding a hand out like they can catch her like a well-timed baseball.

Then the moans start. A blonde woman to the northwest of me starts to rock back and forth and the bodies around me respond. Zombie after zombie moves back and forth while letting out low moans. A female hand with bright red nails shoots out, almost hitting my forehead. I duck and pedal hard.

There are gaps around them, pockets of air and freedom. I swerve into one of these, get the bike straight then rise up on my seat and take a quick glance behind me. If Black Hair has followed me then I can't see him.

The breath sucks out of me when I realize I can't see Cassie anymore, either.

Chapter 13

All I see is zombies. Shuffling, vibrating empty-heads. I'm surrounded. Their ragged, bloodied clothing flaps around them. The reek of blood and decay is everywhere, and I gag and try not to throw up. I take a deep breath, as disgusting as that is, and try not to panic.

What if I fall? What if I fall and that woman right there in the tan business suit tears a chunk off my cheek? What if the guy to my left, the one in the blue jeans and white t-shirt and orange safety vest, digs those big, meaty hands into my stomach and tears out my insides, while all I can do is scream and look up at the mass of faces coming to eat me alive?

This isn't helping.

I take more deep breaths, trying to calm down.

I swerve around a group of zombies, a mottled gray hand reaching out to me like a child trying to grab candy. I keep my balance on the bike, although it's a near thing.

Then, thankfully, the way ahead is clear. Cassie's ten feet ahead of me. I take a deep breath and the tightness in my chest eases.

We exit the mall without any further issues and turn left. We're on a side road that has houses and a few stores.

"Hey, a church!" Cassie points to a one-story, brown-brick church. "There could be adults in there."

"Stop!" I angle my bike in front of hers and cut her off.

It's a large building, sprawling over one entire block. The lawn has long since gone to weeds and there are a few abandoned cars in the parking lot. The doors to the church are shut, and there are no signs of blood or corrupted dead nearby. It sits quietly in the heat like a mirage of a safer world.

"What are you doing?" Cassie frowns.

"Cassie, we can't go in the churches."

"Why not?"

I shake my head. "Whoever was protecting you did you no favors. Churches are risky at best. A lot of the faithful went to them when everything happened. Some people just went in and prayed. Others locked themselves in with the infected without realizing it."

Her eyes widen.

"Then there were the people who thought this

59

was the End of Days. They said it was God's will that we become empty-heads. Some of them walked out into the zombie horde. Others – entire congregations – locked themselves inside their church and turned everyone."

"Oh my gosh," she says, and stares at the church like she can see through the walls to any zombies inside.

My grip tightens on the handlebars as I gaze at the building. There was a woman named Peggy in my apartment complex who spent her Saturdays walking through neighborhoods with her church group, trying to convince people to go to her church. She started every other Saturday by knocking on my door and telling me I should come or else I'd go to Hell. She always clutched her Bible and looked at me sadly, like I might explode into flames on the spot. When the virus reached America, she tried one last time to convince me and my mom to come to her church. I didn't appreciate that she always thought I was going to Hell and that I was a bad person, or that she felt her beliefs were more important than mine, but I *did* appreciate that she thought of me when things went bad.

Her church was one of the first ones to lock down, and one of the few to be broken into back when the local news was still on the air. I don't know if the outbreak in her congregation was accidental or deliberate, but Peggy was one of the zombies who came snarling out of that church at the end.

Cassie and I ride away silently, me thinking about Peggy, and Cassie thinking about who knows what. The area is mercifully low on zombies. I ride past green yards with grass that's a bit high, and some that have already gone to weeds. The houses are those small pretty boxes that were built in the fifties and sixties, with wide steps and porches that look nice but are too hot to use. There are streaks of blood on walls, on cars, and sometimes open doorways with bodies lying in them. The only sounds I hear are the tires on the pavement and the small noises we make while pedaling. I don't hear any birds or cicadas, which is odd for this area in the summer.

After ten minutes, we come to a crossroads. The road to the left leads to more shopping centers and larger, newer subdivisions. The road on the right leads to a quiet country road where the rich people lived.

And in the middle of the hot, black pavement of the crossroads lies what's left of someone I recognize even from ten feet away.

I cry out before I even consider the danger.

Chapter 14

"What?" Cassie asks. I just shake my head.

I jump off my bike and throw it to the ground before I reach his body. I recognize the bottom of his Sketcher sneakers with Dragon Ball Z and other anime characters drawn all over them. In the past year, he'd started to wear his pants so they drooped below his butt, but now they're cinched tight with a belt; I guess so he could run. In the end, he wasn't able to run fast enough. He's wearing a black t-shirt with "Death Note" scrawled in red and black bracelets on his wrists. He was the coolest boy in my class, even though I know not everyone thought so.

I drop to my knees beside him. His eyes are open, fear etched in his face. There's blood all over him. They hadn't eaten much of him, although I'm not sure why they left him alone. He's definitely dead, his eyes staring blankly into the sky at things I can't see, but thankfully he hasn't become a zombie.

I look at his eyes, his blue eyes that glowed whenever he talked about anime and are now dull, and I burst into tears. I cry out loud, making noises I'd only heard come from my mom after the divorce from Dad was final, and he and my brother Mike were far away in California.

Gone.

I fall back onto my butt. Cassie comes up behind me, sits down, and hugs me. I turn around and clutch her tight.

Everyone I've ever known, everyone I've ever loved, is dead. All except this strange little girl who I already like but don't really know.

Thank God my crying doesn't bring any zombies. I don't know why, because I'm beyond loud, but none come. Maybe the universe is giving me a break for once and letting me mourn.

I make Cassie's shoulder sopping wet and I'm sure I almost squeeze the life out of her, but she doesn't complain. Eventually, the sounds quiet and then my tears stop. We sit in silence for a few moments and then Cassie says quietly, "That was Tommy, wasn't it?"

"Yeah." I look over her shoulder, away from the body and toward a lane shaded by gently curving trees. I pull back from her. "I'm sorry."

She gives me a small smile. "It's okay."

Wiping my face, I stand up and walk to my bike,

moving it so I can open my large blue backpack and grab a bottle of water from inside. I drink half of it in one gulp and put it back, then I push and shove in the pack until I find my shimmering blue dress.

I hold it in my hands, watching the light catch. Yes, I'd talked with Tommy about anime, mostly because he was so excited and interested in that. He hadn't asked me to the dance by the time everything started to go bad, but he would have. I would have made that happen.

I stand with the dress in my hands and walk to Tommy. I put it neatly on top of him, but then he looks kind of gay. I wrap his hands around the dress, as if he's holding me. My head feels funny, loose on the inside, and I know I seem crazy, but if Tommy and I can't go to the dance then the dress should be with him. It's the most beautiful thing I've ever owned.

A couple more tears escape and I roughly wipe them away.

"Come on," I say to Cassie, then go to my bike and ride to the shaded lane beyond.

Chapter 15

I remember when we first found out what was happening. Mom called me in to the living room. We'd just had a fight – I wanted to stay out until midnight on Saturday with Tonya, but she said I was too young – so I stood at the entrance and asked, "What?"

My mom sat on our soft, white couch that was patterned with large red and pink roses. On the other side of her, the sliding glass door to our small, second-floor apartment was partially open and the white panels of the plastic, floor-length blinds flapped in the breeze. It was early spring and the weather was pleasantly warm.

"Come sit down," she said. I knew something was up when she didn't even respond to my tone, just patted the couch beside her. I sat down hard, bouncing the couch, but she just hugged me to her body.

I looked at the TV screen and it took a few minutes to absorb what was happening. "Another terrorist attack?"

"Yes and no. Watch," she instructed without even looking at me. Rolling my eyes, I turned my attention to the TV.

There was a bombed-out building with big chunks of concrete everywhere. Bodies lay on the ground and I saw an arm underneath one of the blocks. There were women in flowing saris with blood on them, wailing and crying. The camera moved through the crowd and focused on two people in the middle of the debris. A woman in a beautiful gold and red sari knelt over the body of a man, her feet flexed in her sandals so I saw the soles. God, I hated feet. The camera shifted again, showing her from the side. The man beneath her hands was clearly dead; blood was everywhere, and his black eyes were open and empty.

As I watched, his eyes moved. I gasped, mesmerized as the corpse grabbed the woman's arm and pulled her fiercely to his mouth. Blood spurted from her throat. The crowd screamed and moved back while the cameraman desperately angled for a view. Finally things settled down, revealing the man's body facing the crowd with the woman clearly dead at his feet.

Behind the man, I saw a hand reach out and push

the concrete slab up and over, revealing another male. He was dressed in white, his neck was twisted to one side and a part of his skull was crushed in. He raised a hand and moaned, that haunting moan that hasn't left my ears since.

I screamed.

My mom jumped. She put her hand to her chest and glared at me with her warm, brown eyes.

"Don't do that," she scolded.

"Is this a movie?"

"No, honey, this is CNN. This is live from India." She got up, went to her purse across the room, and pulled out her cell phone as I watched the screen.

The camera was now panning the crowd. I saw something that surprised me, although not as big a surprise as the one I'd just had.

"Hey, Mom, there's a Marine." I pointed at the screen.

"Shhh, honey, I'm on the phone." She waved her hand, telling me to hush. I shrugged and continued watching. The camera had continued moving and the soldier was no longer there.

"Eric, are you watching TV?" Mom was talking to Dad. "Turn on CNN."

She looked at me with the phone to her ear and her eyes filled with horror. "I think this is serious."

I come back to the present with a start. I'm biking down a country lane. The sunshine is bright and the trees lining the paved road on both sides wave gently in the wind. It looks almost normal. But it's Cassie ahead of me on a bike instead of Tonya.

My mom was right. It was serious. But it was, and wasn't, a terrorist attack.

Chapter 16

Firmly back in the present, I pedal hard and catch up to Cassie.

"Hey, Cassie, how did you first hear about all of this? Did you see it on TV?"

"Yeah, I saw it on TV," she replies, but her eyes slide away from mine. Something odd about that.

"Saw it on CNN. India."

"Yeah," Cassie says. "And then all the others."

"And then America."

"I don't want to talk about this, okay? Let's talk about something else."

"Something else…" I repeat, trying to think about a topic. Normally I'd ask her about her family, but then I'd have to talk about mine, and the painful hole in my chest isn't up for that yet.

"What do you like to do for fun?" I ask.

"Play video games, silly." She rolls her eyes at me.

"Anything else? Do you like to play pretend? Maybe be a princess?"

She smiles at me. "Yeah, but not a princess. I like to be a doctor, or a scientist, or a geneticist."

"Really?" I smile. Cassie's blonde hair glints in the sun and her eyes sparkle. I can imagine her getting dressed up in a white coat and performing all sorts of experiments. "Ever blow up your house?"

"No." She giggles. "My dad won't let me have the real stuff yet. I just get to play with safe stuff and some colored liquids."

"Is your dad a scientist then?"

The smile slips from her face. "No, he's more of a doctor. My mom's a marine biologist."

"Wow, that's pretty cool."

"Yeah, this summer my dad was going to get me started on biology."

"Aren't you kind of young for that?"

She makes a noise. "Hey, I can keep up with you."

"I don't doubt that." I use my peripheral vision to glance at her. "You went to private school, didn't you?" I ask.

"No, I was home-schooled. My tutor came three days a week."

Just as I thought, she was friggin' rich and had her own tutor to boot. What does she think of a kid like me? We were middle class before Dad left, but after that money was scarce. I grip my handlebars a bit tighter.

"My mom had me go to soccer for a while, but I sucked at that, so then I went to ballet. I liked it and even made a few friends. Mom said when I first meet people I should just go right up to them, extend my hand, and say 'Hey, I'm Cassie. What's your name?'"

In my school, she would have gotten beaten up for something like that. We never had money for dance classes, or sports for that matter. Not that I was any good at sports. Unless you count running, but I just think it's fun.

"That's cool," I respond.

"How about you? What do you do for fun?"

"Read, watch movies, hang out with friends. Boys." I smile.

"Boys!" She grins at me. "What books do you read?"

"Horror, sci-fi, some fantasy, some adult mainstream. I really like Laurell K. Hamilton, but my mom only let me read a few of those. Something about them being too adult, whatever that means." I roll my eyes. "I really like this series by Rachel Vincent. She writes about werecats, and there's this great love story between the main character and her on-again-off-again boyfriend, Marc. They're deeply in love but she doesn't want to get married."

"Why not?"

"She wants to stay free and young for a while. Really, would you want to get married in your early twenties? No way, that's fun time!"

She shrugs. "Sounds old to me."

Our talk tapers off and we ride in silence. I feel better after talking with Cassie for a bit. She's a cool kid.

It's a beautiful day. The sun shines through the trees, but the leaves shade the road just enough so I'm not hot. It's so nice just to see nature and not see dead bodies everywhere. We're in the rich areas now, so I guess not a lot of people wandered out here. Hopefully Zombie Central is behind us.

I stand up and pump the pedals for a bit, then sit down and coast, turning the bike in wide arcs. Cassie rides next to me, one hand guiding the bike and the other hand on her knee. She looks relaxed.

Together we follow a curve in the road, and after the turn the land on the right clears of trees and has a large green swath of grass. As we get closer, I see a large fenced area full of movement.

"What is that?" Cassie asks.

"I don't know." I shake my head and stand up again, hoping to see better. Unfortunately, I do see more. I sit back down and slow my pace.

"What?"

I'm close enough now that I can see it easily, so I just stop my bike, put both feet on the ground and point. Cassie follows my lead.

The fence consists of very small silver chain links

with that curly barbed-wire at the top. It encloses an area probably about half the size of a football field (hey, I'm not good at measuring distances, okay?).

It also imprisons about thirty zombies.

Chapter 17

"Who would cage zombies?" Cassie asks.

I shrug, still amazed by the sight. They've figured out we're here, of course. As I watch, an empty-head in a bright pink skirt suit shuffles toward us. There is blood all over the front of her and a chunk is missing out of her neck. Her panty hose are torn. Her gait is awkward because she's still wearing one pink high-heeled shoe while the other foot is bare. She reaches for us and moans.

Cassie rolls backward on her bike but I reach out and stop her because I have this odd gut feeling. The pink lady reaches the fence. Her fingers grip the chain links while her body jerks wildly. That's what my gut feeling is about: the fence is electrified. In a few moments, the pink zombie starts to move again, but all she manages to do is shift her fingers a bit and keep frying herself. There are more bodies around the chain links but most of them aren't moving anymore. I guess eventually they either learn to stop or there's a limit to how much electricity even a zombie body can take.

"Come on." I gesture to Cassie. I get off my bike and walk it into the fancy yard, circling to the left around the giant cage. I look over one shoulder and notice Cassie is following me, her mouth a bit open and her eyes focused on the zombie prison.

I walk slowly over the nice grass, leaving a little trail from the bike's tires. By the time I walk around one side of the cage, I see something that makes me stop again, with my mouth wide open.

There's a set of metal bleachers on one side, just like you would find at a middle school football field; a place for parents and friends to sit and watch the game. I look from the bleachers to the cage, and it clicks.

"Oh my God," I say.

"What?" Cassie asks.

"Oh my God, do you get what was happening here?"

Cassie comes to my side and sees the same two items I'm looking at.

"I think they were feeding people to the zombies and watching," I state.

"What?" Cassie asks loudly. She shakes her head. "No way. They were probably just observing them."

"You could do that with plastic chairs and maybe

binoculars. Why the bleachers, Cassie?"

She walks closer to the bleachers.

"Oh God," she says.

Chapter 18

Cassie points to something I can't see, so I walk quickly to her side and look in that direction.

There's a small wooden pen, similar to the one they put bulls into for a rodeo, which feeds directly into the cage.

"Oh God," I echo and sit heavily on the ground, filled with sadness and sickness as we both realize I'm right.

I watch the zombie pen, fighting back tears. *Who were these people? How did they wind up here? How and why were they fed to the zombies? Why were they entertainment?*

A lump forms in my throat and I open my mouth to breathe past it. All of them are dressed nicely: the women in skirts and jackets, the men wearing suits. They could be on their way to church or to work.

As I'm watching, I notice one zombie in particular. He's white, with sandy-blonde hair and pale blue eyes, shuffling very slowly and a bit aimlessly. He wears the remains of a very nice suit, with the sleeves torn off and the bottom of the pants brown from mud, or maybe blood. One of his arms is chewed to bits as if he used it to fend off his attacker. He looks sad, like he knows what has happened to him.

He's also wearing one of those orange bracelets from The Shot.

The Shot (it has some scientific name but nobody calls it that) was developed to decrease the impact of the zombie virus. The goal was to allow people to live and function with the illness, similar to the way the AIDS cocktail works.

"Look! That one had The Shot." I point him out to Cassie. She shoots a glance at him and then goes back to digging into the grass with a twig.

"Did you get it?" I ask her. Neither of us is wearing the orange bracelet. I thought they were ugly, even though with my regular black outfits it gave me this whole wonderful Halloween vibe.

"Yeah." She turns away from me. Okay, not the thing to bring up apparently. But then The Shot was a sore topic with a lot of people, so I let it drop.

I look back at the pen full of zombies and then at the bleachers. The fence is still electrified, so does that mean the people who created this hell are still around? A shiver ripples through me. A zombie I can kind of handle, but these people I really can't. How could they be so sick and so callous?

Cassie throws the stick on the ground and walks to the mansion.

"Cassie, no!" I shout and jump to my feet, running after her. I grab her arm – for once not caring about touching someone without their permission – and stop her.

"What?" she asks.

"That fence is still electrified. Do you really want to take the chance that those people are still around?"

"No," she says quietly, and that's when I notice the tears silently falling down her face.

"It's okay, Cassie." I let go of her arm. God, she was sheltered before, and I led her to this whole nightmare cage and explained it outright. Couldn't I have figured out a way to hide what this was?

I know an adult would just tell her this is the way the world is, but I don't want to tell her that. And looking at the zombies, I realize I no longer have to. I clench my fists.

"Cassie, in the old days I would have told you what adults told me – this is just how the world is, honey." I know that last part sounds bitter and angry, but I can't help it. "They always said the world wasn't fair. But you know what?" I pause.

She looks up at me, waiting for me to finish.

"That's no longer how it is. We can *make* it better now. We can *make* it fair."

Her tears stop and she wipes her face. She grabs my hand and I take her out of there.

#

We're back on the tree-lined road, making slow progress because we're both kind of bummed. The day doesn't seem as pretty or as bright as it did before. Cassie's quiet until we come to a road which branches to the right. She's a bit ahead of me, and she shoots a glance at me over her shoulder then rises up on the pedals to give it all her might as she speeds onto the new road.

"Cassie!" I shout. "Where are you going?" But she ignores me and just keeps up this insane pace. I want to pull out my map and show her this isn't where we're supposed to be going, but I realize she already knows that.

She is way ahead of me as I turn a bend in the road. I reach another bright green lawn, this one smaller than the other one and with a bit of a hill. Cassie's bike lies at the top and she's nowhere in sight.

Chapter 19

"Cassie!" I yell again, but I don't get any kind of response. I hope there aren't any zombies in the area because they're definitely coming otherwise.

I reach the top of the hill and dump my bike next to Cassie's. Straight ahead of me is the back of a large, white two-story house with blue trim. She's left the back door open, so I race past some nice metal patio furniture and then I'm inside.

"Cassie!" I call again, but it's just a waste of time. I'm in a long hallway that runs the length of the house and the front door is open at the other end. I hope she went out that way because this is a huge house to search one room at a time. I pass a kitchen on my right, which is half the size of my mom's apartment, and then just past that is a living room which would finish out the other half. Near the front door is a staircase on the left, with the steps painted white and the rest of it done in the same wood as the floor. It's all very pretty, and very expensive, and it all looks like none of it should be touched.

I run out of the front door and down three white steps. There's a half-circle of cement at the bottom of the stairs, leading to a sidewalk and a graveled driveway. I stop, hands on my hips, breathing hard through my open mouth. Halfway across the green expanse of lawn to my right, Cassie is staring at a lump on the ground.

"Delilah?" she asks, and her voice is quiet, shaky. God, she sounds scared. This is my brave friend, who runs into potentially zombie-infested alleys with a whoop, and she is scared.

"Delilah, will you please go look at –" she stops for a moment – "go over there and see who that is? Will you please see if it's a man with a gold ring on his hand, with an inscription?"

And then it all clicks. This is Cassie's house and that might be her father out there.

"Sure," I answer softly.

I know she's watching as I walk slowly out to the body. The grass here is torn up and trampled on. As I get closer, I slide my knife into my hand, trying to hide it from Cassie, but getting it out just in case. I stop just out of range and wait for movement.

The lump is a man dressed in tan pants, a blue shirt and reddish brown shoes. He's white with blonde hair like Cassie's. He's lying on his side and he looks battered, with one leg and one arm at odd angles. Something about his face doesn't look quite right, either. Slowly, I move to where his eyes should be able to see me, but there's no movement in response. They're filled with blood and have tiny pinpricks of blue in the middle. I take his wrist and lay him on his back, even though it takes some work. There's a huge bullet hole in his forehead and he's covered in gore.

Except for the hole, he looks a bit like Gina, our neighbor from the apartment complex across the street who my mom and I helped 'disappear' one night into a woman's shelter. He looks battered.

I glance back at Cassie then kneel on the ground next to the man. From the condition of the grass and his body, I think he was beaten up and then shot. Someone murdered him. Crap.

I notice the gold band on one of his fingers, and although it weirds me out to do it, I slide the ring off. There's an inscription inside: "Love is family, family is love." I wrap my hand around it and walk to Cassie.

I give her the ring, and she collapses to the ground with a scream that's a cry and a moan all wrapped in one.

Chapter 20

When this happened to me, back on that road at the start of the day, Cassie hugged me without asking, so I think it's okay for me to do the same thing. I've barely had time to sit down and she's in my lap and hugging me, crying. I pat her hair like my mom would do for me while I look over her shoulder watching for zombies, just in case.

After a while, she calms down enough that I get her inside. I shut the door behind us and go into the living room. We sit on the couch and she wraps around me again even though that one shoulder is still wet. Ick. But she did it for me, so I sit still and pat her.

Eventually, the tears stop flowing and I realize she's fallen asleep. *Is it okay for me to move now?* But I don't want to risk waking her up, so I stay.

We're sitting on a white couch that has large pink roses printed on it. It's softer than cardboard but still isn't as comfortable as some of the broken-down couches I've sat on. There's a gorgeous, dark wood coffee table in front of me and the far wall has the largest flat-screen TV I've ever seen. To my left is a small window, and in front of the window are two large, cushy chairs in the same pink rose pattern as the couch. They're clustered around a small wood table with a chessboard on top. The wall to my right is lined with bookcases, filled with books instead of knick-knacks.

The only thing that shows use besides the obviously mid-game chess set is the giant coffee table book resting on the table in front of me. It's a history of Egypt, and there are little yellow sticky notes stuck to various pages. I try to reach for the book, because I'm fascinated by ancient Egypt (okay, I'm a bit of a geek, and I know history isn't cool, but they built the pyramids thousands of years ago, for God's sake!), but I can't get to it without shifting Cassie and potentially waking her up.

So I'm just sitting there in silence, actually about to drift off when I hear a noise in the other room.

My sleepiness is burned off by adrenaline in seconds. I'd like to believe it's just a cat in the other room, with no question as to how it survived, but I know better. I look down at Cassie. I really don't want to wake her up, which I know is ridiculous because there's a zombie in the other room, but really it's been so nice. So I put a pillow over her ears – that will help with the noise, right? – and reach across my body with my right hand to unclip the gun at my side.

I cock the weapon like I've seen on TV and point it at the door. Really, how hard could this be?

Moments tick by and my arm starts to hurt. What's taking so long?

I put my arm down and of course that's when it appears at the door.

I'm expecting maybe someone in a maid's uniform or a butler's outfit, but instead it's some guy in a polo shirt and khakis. Is that the new uniform? I don't know. His neck's been ravaged, and it's not holding up too well; there's a lot of red and green and then some squirming white things I'd rather not think about. His hand grips the remains of a gold doorknob. I don't what that's about.

As I raise the gun again, his head turns to me, and his cracked brown eyes widen in surprise. He moans and raises his hand just as I squeeze the trigger.

Nothing happens.

Crap!

What the hell is wrong with my gun?!

Chapter 21

It takes me a few moments and then I remember something about a safety. I mess with the gun until I think I've found it. Of course by this time he's in the room, but ha-ha, I've figured it out. I pull the trigger and the noise is so loud I swear I've exploded the house.

And I miss him completely. Apparently it's not as easy as they make it look on TV.

He moans again and now he's only a foot away. Cassie's awake and I rudely throw her to the floor, dropping the gun and grasping with my left hand for anything I can take. I find a lamp, turn it to the side and put my whole body into a swing just like I would a bat. It makes some impact, causing the zombie to stumble a bit, and then the gun goes off again.

I turn and look at Cassie, who's holding the pistol in both hands.

"I can't believe you just shot at me," I say, giving her a dirty look so hopefully she'll realize that shooting in my direction is a bad idea. I hit the zombie again and he stumbles backward but the lamp breaks in two.

I search for a weapon, and fortunately Cassie's decided to stop shooting at me because she throws my bat to me. Armed again, I hit the zombie in the stomach with all of my strength. I follow up with a hit to the skull, but the friggin' empty-head still won't fall down. I aim once more and Cassie runs over and tackles its legs at the same time as I'm hitting it. Finally, it's down and I make a mess of the head until it stops moving.

I drop the bat, breathing hard. This is too much work. I've got to figure out how to shoot that gun effectively.

"I want you to bury my dad," Cassie says.

"Cassie, it's not safe." I gesture at the body near the door. "Is that a butler's uniform, by the way?"

She frowns at me. "No, that's one of the neighbors."

It hits me that's she just casually talked about a person she knew, that we killed... the, uh... body of, together, like it was Tuesday.

"I know it's dangerous, but it's safer here than near the mall. We can see them coming. I'll keep watch."

"Cassie, that's a lot of work."

She turns tightly on one heel and walks out of the room. A few seconds later, I hear a door slam. I'm sitting on the couch wondering whether to go after her when the door bangs open and she appears in the doorway holding a shovel. Cassie simply stares at me, with no sign of light or happiness in her face at all, just shut down and determined.

I push myself off the couch, grab an afghan off a nearby chair, and take the shovel.

"Watch everything," I order.

I walk ahead of her and cover most of him with the afghan. Once I'm done with that she comes nearer and keeps watch. I start digging.

I make a very shallow grave, but even with that by the time I'm done my arms are shaking so badly I can barely hold the shovel.

"Will that cover him?" she asks, and I look up at her from the bottom of my eyes, dead tired. "Okay." She holds her hands up. "Look away." I don't want her to see me move him. It's going to be very awkward. A breeze blows across my skin and I stop for a second, enjoying the cool air. I shut my eyes for a moment.

I open them and drop the shovel to the ground. I set the afghan aside then make sure Cassie isn't watching me. Then I roll, drag and push her father's body into the ground. It just barely fits.

I drape the blanket over him and pull it up under his chin. I think she needs to see him, to really know inside that he's gone, but I'm worried it will give her nightmares. I close his eyes, try to cover the worst of what happened to his face, and then stand up and brush my hands against my jeans.

"Okay, Cassie," I say.

She turns slowly and looks into the grave. She bursts into tears again, and I want to go hold her but we need to face each other so we can look out for zombies in both directions.

"Why don't you say something?" I ask softly. She just cries harder. I sigh and bow my head.

"Today, we lay Cassie's father to rest. He was a good man, greatly loved by his daughter. She will miss him and love him always."

I grab some dirt and put it in Cassie's hand. "Throw it in there," I tell her.

She tosses it limply.

"I love you, Daddy," she says softly, tears flowing down her face as she grabs my hand with her dirty one.

The breeze kicks up again, making my hair whip softly against my neck. I notice she smells a bit like apples, and I wish, I really wish I could make her dad alive and well again, just to see her smile.

Chapter 22

After the burial, I stumble back inside the house. There's no way we can go further today.

Together, we go through the house and make sure it's locked and zombie-free. The home is big, empty and beautiful. As we sit on tall chairs at the kitchen counter, eating cold food out of cans, I imagine Cassie is surrounded by memories. She doesn't talk me to me and barely pays attention to her food. She just stares off into space and shovels corn into her mouth.

When we're finished I collect our dishes and put them in the sink, even though there isn't any way for me to wash them. As the forks clink in the stainless steel bottom, I think that it was really nice to eat food with a utensil again even if said food was cold.

I lead Cassie upstairs to a hallway that has lush, white carpet that doesn't even have a mushed-down part in the middle where people have walked on it a lot. She turns away from me, opening one of the doors, and then pauses as if remembering I'm here.

"The guest room is down the hall and to the right." She points and then is closed off in her bedroom.

"Cassie," I say to the closed door. "Come get me if you need anything, okay?"

I tell myself she's acting like this because she's sad, and not because she doesn't want to be around me.

I walk down the hall and open the first door to the right. It's a pretty nice room, about the size of my mom's master bedroom in the apartment. All of the furniture is light brown; obviously all from a matching set which was bought at the same time. There's a dresser along the wall to my right, with four long drawers and nice round handles. The bed is parallel to me with the headboard against the next wall. It's huge - three pillows wide – and is covered with a white bedspread with elegant little purple flowers on it. There's a mosquito net thingy which starts at the ceiling and drapes over the entire bed.

The wall across from it has a flat-screen TV flanked by two bookcases, and again the bookcases have books in them. I shut the door behind me, put my backpack on the floor, and examine the shelves. They're filled with paperbacks ranging from thrillers, to romances, to science fiction; a truly thoughtful, wonderful selection varied enough for any guest. I sigh and look at the TV. I would have really liked to have stayed here in the past. Cassie's parents had style.

Just for the fun of it, I grab one of the thrillers and crawl onto the bed with my bat. Then I read until I fall asleep.

#

When I wake up Cassie is already up and about, her eyes still puffy and her skin pale. We eat brunch and afterwards she puts down her fork and stares ahead as she talks to me.

"Thank you for burying my dad. I'm glad we stayed the night, but I want to get a few things and then go, okay?" She drops her head and glances up at me.

"Okay," I answer. It's selfish, but I'm glad she wants to leave. I'm also grateful that for all of the hurt in her that she's still strong enough to keep going.

"Do you need my help getting the stuff?"

"I could probably fill another backpack with what I'd like to bring, but some of it I can replace when we get to a safe place. How about you just come with?"

"Sounds good." I smile.

She leads me down some raw-wood stairs to the concrete floor of the basement. It looks like any other, full of junk, cardboard boxes and a washing machine. Then I follow her to the back of the room and a large metal door. There is a small pad set in the wall to the left of it. It looks like one of those thumbprint checkers from spy movies.

Cassie reaches down her shirt and pulls out a key on a string necklace. She inserts it into a lock above the doorknob.

"He had the lock put in two weeks after we first heard about the zombies, even though everyone started complaining about the compromised security. Then, a few weeks before he – before I left, he gave me a copy of the key. I didn't know why at the time."

"Your father?"

She nods and opens the door. Cassie lets me walk inside and then locks the door behind me.

Chapter 23

We're in a lab, much like the ones in school, only a lot nicer, with clean, white countertops and shining sinks. Laptops are placed around the room in convenient places, situated nicely away from working areas. I realize that I can see everything clearly, which means the electricity is on because the room is windowless. It takes me a minute to locate a generator neatly hidden under one of the counter areas.

"I came down here last night," Cassie says. I wonder then hope she didn't sleep down here.

"It's nice." I don't really know what else to say. Cassie nods and walks to one of the laptops on the far side of the room. She quickly has it humming, pulling a thumb drive out of her pocket and plugging it in.

"It'll be just a few minutes," she tosses over her shoulder. I walk around as she works, running my fingertips along the smooth, slick surface of the countertop. Past Cassie is a white door with a top half made of that cloudy, white glass that seems to exist mostly in old school buildings. I'm just reaching for the doorknob when Cassie says, "Don't go in there." There's a hardness to her voice I haven't heard before, a bit of confidence mixed with a commanding tone. I'm back by her side before I even realize it.

"What are you doing?" I ask.

"Getting some files. I'll take some of the lab books, but I like having the electronic copies, too."

"Files of what?"

Her flying fingers hover over the keys. "I suppose I can trust you, because you saved my life, and telling you won't break the security because the government doesn't exist anymore."

She visibly braces herself and avoids my eyes. "It's the data from developing The Shot, and the research he did after we found out it didn't work."

"Your dad developed The Shot?" I screech, waving my arms without looking and sweeping a beaker to the floor with a crash. She flinches.

"Yes," she replies softly.

"Do you know how many people sold things very precious to them –" and here my voice breaks – "just so they could get The Shot?"

"Yes."

"Do you know what it was like to see people you cared about die in front of you because they thought they were protected?" I know I'm shouting, but I can't help it, just like I can't stop the tears flowing down my face.

"No," she says quietly. "I'm sorry. It was never supposed to be a cure."

"Then why the price! Why a thousand dollars per shot?" I yell. "Why set it so high that it tore families apart and left mothers and fathers hungry?"

I turn away from her, crying openly now and full of rage. I smash a whole set of beakers.

"We tried! My dad argued with them. He said it should be free, but they wouldn't listen!"

Tears are forming in her eyes and I can tell she's upset, but I can't stop. I glance around for something else to smash but all of the beakers are now a glittering mess. Cassie puts a counter between us.

"He didn't have any bodies when he started working on it. After the attacks, they still refused to give us any. For months afterwards, we just got vials of blood they promised were infected."

"After the attacks?"

She nods, her face somber. "They had him looking for the cure weeks before India."

"Oh my God." A wave of nausea washes away my anger. "The Marine I saw at the attack. Did the government cause this? Did they create the zombie virus?"

"They never said yes to that. The most they would admit was they knew this might happen a few months before they came to my dad and a few months before India. They knew. A handful of other countries knew, too."

"Dear God," I mutter, my hands cold and clammy with the knowledge that I may have been right.

Chapter 24

I walk away and let her work. Then what she said triggers another thought in my head, one I'm not about to share with her.

The way her father's body had looked... now it strikes me that maybe he'd been assassinated, killed by an angry mob. I don't want to ask, but I have the feeling he saved her life by sending her off with someone else while he confronted them, even though it meant he would die.

I run my hand along the cool countertops, realizing he died to save Cassie. His actions, his ring, and her response to his death all tell me he did that out of love. But he also kept alive the one other person who knew about his research, potentially saving all of us.

I turn and look at Cassie's back. What are the chances that I would run into maybe the one person left who could save the world? Surely there are more like her out there, right? With that kind of knowledge? What if there aren't?

I'd gotten good grades in school. Maybe I can help? And hey, it isn't like I'm going to get to be a famous actress now.

"Cassie, can I help?"

"What?" She looks up, a bit distracted.

"Can I help with the research?" I take a breath. I can't believe I'm going to offer up this next part; I so want to be in an area where I can kill zombies I don't know. "Since everything's set up here, we could stay here and work on it."

She stops working, blinking several times and tipping her head back, then shakes her head. "No, ah –" her voice dips low – "you were right. Let's get out of town. Away from everywhere we knew. We can set up a lab somewhere else. And then yes, I'd like your help. You definitely have more science than I have." She tries to smile, but it breaks in the middle and never reaches her eyes.

"Cool."

"I'm almost done here. Why don't you get everything else ready?"

"Sure," I say quietly and slip out of the room.

#

A few hours later, I find her in her bedroom. It's a typical little girl's room, the walls a dark pink color with white trim. There are pictures of unicorns on the wall and Barbies piled in a heap in a wire crate. Her giant four-poster bed is covered in a bedspread with ballerinas all over it, twirling on one toe forever.

Then there's the rich part. She has a tan chest of drawers with a TV on top – a TV, for goodness sake! – and what looks like a satellite receiver. Next to that is a tan desk with a laptop and two large flat-screen monitors, with school books piled next to the computer. I notice that the books all seem to be science-oriented – again, she's smart.

"I'm almost done," she says, and shuts down her laptop.

"Do you want to bring that?"

"No, too heavy. I'll pick up a new one wherever we settle down. I've got everything important anyway." She holds up a silver thumb drive.

"Okay," I agree as she leads the way out of the room. At the last moment, I take a picture off her chest of drawers. Cassie's sitting on a chair with a big bright smile, and a man and woman stand behind her with smiles to match, one hand from each on her shoulders. I remove the picture from the frame and slip it into her backpack when she's not looking.

I know from experience that it's easier when you can remember what they looked like.

Chapter 25

I love driving a car. I love the freedom and the power. I love how you push down the pedal and the car responds to you.

I really don't know why Cassie is screaming.

Okay, she's not yelling but she's definitely buckled up and scrunched in her seat. She looks tense. "I'm just having a little fun, okay?"

"Watch the road." She points in front of us as I swerve. I smile the whole time.

It was my decision to take the car. We'd been riding along on our bikes and there it was, in the middle of the road, door open and inviting. Someone had left the keys in it. Cassie said it probably wouldn't start, and I'd agreed with her – I mean, I would have left it running while I went to go do whatever – but they'd nicely shut it off before they ran away, and they never returned. We fit the bikes in the trunk (okay, tied the trunk down) and took off.

The nice thing about the pretty country road is there are only a few abandoned cars. Occasionally we hit little pockets of car clumps, sometimes with the vehicles spread willy-nilly across the road and sometimes with all of them parked nicely to one side.

Every now and then I drive past a car that's all on its own; usually with blood-streaked windows. That makes me a bit sad, wondering things like how close had they come to getting out? Where were they now?

The ones with zombies trapped inside are an easy story to figure out.

I slow down a little and stop voluntarily weaving all over the place to give Cassie a break. She sighs and slowly relaxes as she starts to trust me.

"Hey, Cassie, could you get my purse?"

"Sure." She reaches in the back and pulls it into her lap.

"In the front pocket is a thumb drive. Go ahead and plug it into the stereo, please." I motion to the USB port on the front. She plugs it in. I turn on the stereo and fill the sedan with the sounds of Lady Gaga.

Cassie whoops and we both start car dancing. What the heck; no one can see us. She rolls down the window and puts her hand out, letting it hang in the breeze for a while, and then doing that up-down wave swoop thing.

I smile and whoop, too, doing my little car dancing thing while still maintaining control of the car. The sun is shining, the bright blue sky is dotted by white fluffy clouds, I'm warm and driving a car, and there isn't a zombie in sight.

Life is good.

#

I went on a trip like this with my mom once. That was the first time I got to drive. Things had been so bad at home, and it felt so good to get away from all of that, to get out into the bright sunshine and just drive. It was great to drive away from the troubles, and to be in a special place where we got to do fun and special things because we were on vacation. Oh, and how good it felt to have Mom all to myself, talking about books and movies and food, and fun times in her life, and fun memories we had.

I remember just hanging out with her, just like Cassie and I were now, and enjoying the moment.

I didn't enjoy the trip back as much because I'd learned that my life was changing forever. My mom and dad were getting divorced, and Dad and Mike were moving out to California.

Everything gone, everything changed, but at least we had that bright moment in the car under the sun.

The next morning I wake up slowly, comfortably warm under a light blanket on the backseat. I don't move, really; I just kind of open my eyes and take in the world. I feel safe and good, surrounded by the soft gray of the fabric covering the seats. The windows are cracked open a bit to let in fresh air, and just past them I see a bright blue sky without any clouds at all.

I also see a zombie shuffling slowly past the car.

Chapter 26

I open my mouth in shock but manage not to gasp. It hasn't heard me, and since I didn't move it hasn't seen me either. *God, please don't let Cassie wake up.*

My eyes flick to the front to see her in the passenger seat facing me with her eyes wide open. I know from her expression that they are walking past my side of the car, too.

Dear God, we're in the middle of a slow-moving zombie parade.

In horror, I watch as more and more pass. A man goes by with a huge flap of skin hanging from his face, exposing the muscle beneath. After him is a woman in a flowered sundress, looking steadily forward, with a baby carrier strapped to her back. It takes everything I have not to move, not to scream, as the baby in that backpack turns its head my way and grins, its cracked green eyes glowing and no other sign of the virus visible. I can't see how it died.

It turns its head in the other direction and they pass on while my heart jumps in my chest like a panicked rabbit.

God, it would be so much easier if I could just close my eyes, but they might see it. Under the blanket, I clench my fists and I feel a bit better.

A male zombie in a formerly white tank top walks into the side of the car, rocking it a bit, and I bite my tongue to keep from screaming. His slack face turns to the car, his disinterested face that would grin as it tore my body apart. I can feel his teeth on me; I can hear my screams fall on his deaf ears as he tears me apart.

Oh, God. Oh, God, please get me out of this. Please get us out of this.

I blur my vision and try to just ignore everything. I try not to think about the unfeeling death moving around us like a pride of lions, so close to their prey without even realizing it.

Would the car be able to protect us? Can their fingers fit through the small breach left by the open windows and use that leverage to break the glass?

Are we like Twinkies just waiting to be opened?

Oh, God. Oh, God. Oh, God.

Oh, God, what if they bunch up? What if a mass of them try to pass us by?

See, I can't even breathe deep and slow this panic down. If I could just shut my eyes… Okay, I'll try to just think of something calming, or happy.

But oh, God, if I do that I won't be ready to leap into action if they do attack. Crap. Okay, if this goes down, then I'll scramble as fast as I can into the driver's seat and get the car going. It's small but surely it could mow some of them down, enough to get free, right?

Under the blanket, I wriggle my hand into my jeans pocket. It's a tight fit and I can't move around. Slowly, slowly, I manage to get my fingers into my pocket and pull out the keys.

Thank God. Okay, I'm ready and I have a plan. May my soul find my family and loved ones if this doesn't work out.

Chapter 27

Thankfully, I never have to put my plan in place. I don't know how long it lasts, but eventually the parade thins and then stops. I wait for a long time after I see the last one, trying to make it like maybe twenty minutes or so, but odds are it's really only five minutes.

Eventually, I sigh and look at Cassie. Her eyes are closed and one hand is on her forehead. "Cassie?" I whisper. "Cassie, are you good?"

She opens her eyes and takes a deep breath just like I did. "Yeah, I think so."

"I'm gonna come over the seat and get us out of here, okay?"

"That sounds good. Just don't go wherever they went."

"Yeah." I grin. I climb over the console between the seats and settle into the driver's seat. I put the key in the lock, place my hands on the steering wheel, and I feel in control again. No adult ever mentioned to me the feeling of power and dominion you can get from driving a car.

Once we're going, I raise all of the windows from the buttons by my left arm and crank the AC. I accelerate to thirty miles an hour; I want some speed but I don't want to roar up on the parade without any warning. Fortunately, I see an off-ramp that leads to a side road and I take it, thinking I can effectively pass the zombies without alerting them that we're there.

I hit the bottom of the exit and zoom through a defunct, darkened light. I accelerate until I hit fifty. Within minutes I can see the horde of zombies on the freeway to my left, but fortunately I'm right and we're far enough away that they don't even turn their heads.

"God, that's just not right. Where do you think they're going?" Cassie's turned to the side so she can stare past me and watch the slow-moving empty-heads.

I shrug. "Who knows? Maybe they got the scent of a huge group of humans, or maybe they're establishing a territory? I don't know a lot about the behavior of large packs of predators, but from what I've seen they're operating on some sort of instincts."

I could feel Cassie's eyes on me. "Delilah, that's one of the smartest things you've said."

I feel a bit of a smile creeping over me. "I'm an artsy type, and I hang out with a lot of artsy types. They didn't necessarily like it when I seemed interested in regular school stuff. But you seem like you might be okay with it." I sneak a sideways glance at her, just to check, and I'm glad to see her nodding.

"There might be a scientist in you." She grins.

"Nah, let's not get too wild. I'm still into the acting thing, and I'm probably not bright enough anyways."

Cassie shrugs and turns on the music again. "Hey, do you think they dance?"

"The zombies? Sad as it is, probably not." I glance over at the bodies we're speeding by, and I hope that whatever's in there, the instincts and whatnot, that none of it includes a trapped soul. *Please, let them just be driven by pure animal instinct, even if it means they can't appreciate music and they can't dance.*

Now that I'm safe in a car, I wish them as painless an existence as possible.

#

By the middle of the afternoon, we've left the freeway for a two-lane highway. It will take longer to get to Colorado this way, but we'll have more choices if anything comes up – like a group of zombies – unlike the freeway where our main choices for detours are concrete barriers and overpasses.

So I'm zooming along at a good eighty miles an hour, listening to Crystal Method and letting it speed my blood like an electric super train. Then I come over a hill and realize way too late that there's a giant hole in the middle of the road.

And unlike the movies, we don't happily go sailing over the gap and come out okay on the other side.

Chapter 28

One moment, there's pavement under my tires and the next, Cassie and I are screaming. There's this wonderful feeling of weightlessness then I'm waking up with the feeling that a bit of time has passed, and I find myself still strapped in the front seat and the car firmly on the ground.

I push the airbag away from me, noting that the back of my neck, my right knee, and my forearm all hurt but other than that, I seem fine. Of course, I haven't tried getting up yet. Slowly I turn my head to the side, and then pull the other airbag away from Cassie. There's a cut on her forehead but I can't see anything other than that.

"Cassie," I say but she doesn't move. I reach down and unbuckle myself then shake her a bit. "Cassie."

She screams.

"Are you hurt?"

She looks at me confused for a bit, then blinks her eyes and shakes her head. I grab a pillow from the backseat. "Here, hold this to your head. You're bleeding."

She looks at me weird but she does it, and I adjust her placement until it's just right. Then I try to get an idea of where we are.

About a block ahead of me is a dirt and rock face, and above that are bits of the blacktop from the highway. The crevice we're in is shaped like a fish and consists of rocks, dirt and bits of concrete. I shift around to look out the back and that's when the adrenaline starts pumping through my system, burning like acid.

"Oh, crap," I mutter quietly. "Cassie, we need to get out of here right now."

Slowly, she turns in her seat to see what I'm looking at. On the far side of the crevice is an entire group of zombies huddled together. I have no idea why they're in a little clump, and I really don't want to find out.

"Are you unbuckled?"

"Yeah."

"Crawl out my side."

"Where are we going?" Cassie's voice is high.

I look around. "There." I point to where the slope is milder. It looks like hills I've gone up before; challenging, but doable. I think the zombies haven't gotten out because they simply can't plan well enough to map a route up that face.

"Just follow me up. You'll do fine," I tell her when I see how big Cassie's eyes are, but she just nods. "Okay, let's do this," I state and open the door.

I take off running like a crack addict. I'm halfway to the rock face when I realize Cassie isn't by my side. She's still struggling to get out of the car. I stop and wave my hands at her, but she's focused on something on her foot so she doesn't notice. Should I run to her? I glance quickly at the zombies, and fortunately they still haven't noticed we're there.

Suddenly, she shoots free and falls on the ground with a loud thump. We both look toward the zombies, and yup, one of them is turning this way.

I run in a quick, high burst to Cassie's side, yank her up off the ground, and hold her wrist as I race us back to the rock face.

"Delilah," she hisses. She yanks her wrist free and drops a step behind me, just as I hear the moan.

Chapter 29

I can't help it. I turn my head and look even though I know I shouldn't.

He's a big, fat meaty zombie, his belly large and rounded over his pants, and he's pointing one huge, hairy arm at us. Bloodstains are around his face and at various points on his green striped shirt. I don't know what he's been eating exactly, but he's still chewing as he moans at us, and it is one of the grossest things I've seen.

"Oh, God," I whisper then realizing noise levels don't matter anymore, I shout, "Run!"

I turn my attention back to my feet, and then I'm up the first part of the slope and on to the harder, slower part. I dig my hands and get a good hold, and find that Cassie's just below me. The zombies are uncurling from their circle and Big and Meaty is already headed over here in his slow, frightening fashion.

This is the first time I've climbed under any kind of pressure.

I turn back to the face. The slope is at a tighter angle than I'd like, and there are lots of little rocks that keep sliding downhill at the slightest touch. There isn't a way to go straight up; instead, I will need to go a bit to the left, and then a bit northeast, and then turn, and keep doing that until we zigzag our way up to the top. It's doable.

I dig in and feel that peace that comes from concentrating; the same sense of calm I get from running or climbing. I reach out and a bit of the surface slides beneath my fingers. I think I have a hold but I slide a tiny bit instead, my fingertips sweating in response and my heart jumping. I grab a better spot, dig my feet into the side and shift myself safely into the position I'd like. Then I do it again.

I'm maybe a fourth of the way from the top when Cassie screams.

I anchor myself on my side, and then watch in horror as she slides down the face. Big and Meaty is trying to scramble up to her, his huge palms reaching for her.

If he gets her, he will tear her apart before I touch the ground.

"Dig your feet in! Grab anything!" I shout at her. She's panicking; I can see it in her eyes. "There - there's a big rock coming up – grab it!"

"I can't," she cries.

"Yes, you can!" I shout in my baddest, toughest voice.

She reaches out, slides past the rock, and grabs the edge at the last moment. Big and Meaty jumps and swipes at her sneakers then falls back down the slope just as Cassie screams.

"Scrunch your feet up!"

She digs them into the slope beneath her.

"Good! Now take a deep breath, in and now out. Forget the zombies. Just think about the rocks. Think about where you're going to go. If you slide, it's okay; just look for another rock."

I see her calm down. Cassie looks up at me, and her face is dirty with rock dust and tear tracks.

"It's okay, honey. It's going to be okay. Just concentrate on finding your path."

She's still crying, but I see her focus on the rocks. She listens to me and fights her fear, and slowly but surely she makes her way up the slope. By the time she slides over the top her whole body is shaking, but she still makes it over.

We lie on the blacktop and Cassie throws an arm over her face, crying and laughing at the same time.

I pat her elbow. "You did a fantastic job."

She moves her arm off her face, and I can see she's stopped crying. "Thanks. Do you think we're safe?" She motions her head toward the pit.

"I think so." I turn over onto my stomach, slide

back to the edge, and look down into the crevice.

Big and Meaty stands at the bottom and stares up at us with the patience of the dead. He's given up on getting up the slope, but he hasn't given up on us. The rest of the zombies, however, are already back in their odd little circle at the other end.

"We're fine."

Cassie wiggles up next to me and we examine them from a safe distance.

"How do you think they got in there?"

"Don't know." I shrug. "I'm wondering if someone drove them in."

"How would you herd a bunch of zombies?"

"I don't know. It just seems like it would be neat if someone had gotten an extra twenty zombies out of the way."

"Yeah. They probably just fell in, though."

"Wouldn't they know to avoid a gaping hole?"

"We didn't." Cassie grins.

"Hey, we were going eighty miles an hour when we hit that gap."

"Exactly." She giggles.

We watch the zombies for a while. Then I get thirsty and reach for a bottle of water out of my backpack. "Darn it."

"What?"

"Everything we have – my backpack and yours– is down there, with the zombies."

Chapter 30

"That's okay," Cassie says. "We'll just get more supplies in town."

I think of the picture of her mom and dad in her pack, but instead I say, "Like the research?"

"Oh." She frowns.

"Unless you have one of the drives on you?"

She shakes her head. I stare at the broken mass of my pretty car. "I'll go back down and get just the packs. We can pick up new bikes somewhere else."

"I'll go," Cassie counters, and she's actually got a leg over the side before I grab her arm.

"No, Cassie. I can get up the slope quicker."

"But I know what I'm doing now."

"No. I have a bigger reach and I'll be quicker. Plus, those backpacks are going to be heavy."

She thinks for a minute and then sits down again. "Okay."

I examine the situation. Big and Meaty has gone

back to the zombie huddle, but even if I slide all the way down he'll probably be able to meet me at the car. I've got my gun and my knife, but Cassie's gun is in her pack, and mine only has a small number of bullets.

I'll be dead before I can get back to the slope.

"We passed a town right before we hit the pit. How about we go there, get some supplies, and then come back and get the packs?"

"Supplies?"

"Well, like lunch, water, new bikes, maybe something like a rope or a bucket, and then something to distract the zombies."

"Sure. How far away was it?"

"Beats me. Can't be far, though."

So we head back, along the same road I once raced so grandly on, just at a much slower pace.

Screw the bikes. I want my car back.

#

A few hours later and I am sticky-hot, my feet hurt and I'm tired. That bright blue sky sure looks pretty until you're stuck under it for an extended length of time. The sound of cicadas has become annoying. There isn't any shade at all, just miles and miles of baked grass; sometimes on a flat surface and sometimes gently rolling hills. The only good thing is that we haven't seen any zombies along the way. I just want to lie down in a room pumped full of air conditioning and fall asleep.

"Are we there yet?" Cassie jokes.

"No," I snap. It would've been a funny question to ask if I wasn't frigging hot and fed up with this whole walking thing.

We head up a small hill I don't even remember from our trip out here. As I top the rise, there, finally, I can see the outskirts of town. I collapse on the grass. "We're here. Let's look at it a minute." Cassie nods and sits beside me.

We get lucky in a way. The first thing we'll hit is a shopping center, one of those huge ones that's basically an outdoor mall. There's a SuperMart, a Home Depot, a Barnes and Noble, a Ross, a PetSmart, and non-chain clothing stores between each. Chain restaurants dot the parking lot. Oh, and did I mention there's like a thousand frickin' zombies down there?

"What weapons do we have?" I ask.

It turns out we each have a knife. I also have a gun with six bullets in it, which I'm not very good at shooting. Boy, do I wish I had a bat.

"So, what first?"

"I would kill for a soda, chips and a hamburger." I grin at my own joke.

"Yeah, right," Cassie says. "Do we go for weapons or food first?"

"How about both?" I point to the SuperMart. There are currently at least twenty zombies milling around just outside the entrance.

Some of the empty-heads cluster around the store openings as if something reminds them that those doors might open and people might pour out. Handfuls wander among the dead people and the dead cars, looking for food or other zombies or whatever. Then there are random groups standing away from the stores, like they're camping out and waiting for some huge event.

I spot a female carrying a huge plastic bag from the shoe store. Sometimes it's like, when they zombify, they forget themselves so totally they don't even notice they're still carrying things they can put down, and those items become like a weird extra body part. Imagine that, going through the undead life carrying a bag of shoes you would never remember to wear.

I wonder if she'd been excited about the shoes; if she couldn't wait to get home and wear them with her favorite outfit. She must have been one of the first killed in this area. I can't imagine anyone going shoe shopping in those final days.

I wonder what day was the tipping point, when the day before it had been perfectly reasonable to buy shoes and the next, it would have been outrageous because you were now running for your life. I don't remember which day exactly had been the transition.

"Delilah?"

"Yeah?"

"So, are we going to go?"

I snap out of my thoughts. "Sure. How should we get there?"

"Let's just go." Cassie stands up.

"No," I shake my head. "We have very few weapons. Let's plan." She sits back down and I look at the situation. "What about the backside? You know, where the deliveries come in? Surely there won't be a lot of them there?"

"Don't those usually have solid doors? How would we get in?"

I pick up the gun and shrug. "I shoot the lock."

"Okay." Cassie agrees. Then we're off, descending into the biggest mass of zombies we've faced so far.

Chapter 31

We skirt around to the back, moving very slowly so none of the zombies catch sight of us. Thankfully none of them have wandered there; I guess it's as boring to the dead as it is to the living.

The SuperMart is the huge box store in the middle, and I jog at a good pace until reaching that area. It may be empty back here, but I still don't want to get caught. The heat blazes down on me, made worse by the black road and the white walls of the stores.

All of the doors are dark gray and look heavy and solid from the outside. I go up to one of them, Cassie right by my side, and notice something odd.

"It's open," she whispers. The gray door is damaged. *This wasn't left open by a fleeing employee; it's been forced open by someone. I don't think a zombie could have done this; it had to have been a living human, but then why did they leave it open? Had they gotten it open only to be eaten right after they went inside?*

I slip my knife into my hand and whisper, "Be careful."

I slide around the open door and take a step to one side so Cassie can fit inside, too. I wait for my eyes to adjust, fearing there will be a body at my feet and a moaning zombie on the other side, but as the room reveals itself I see only shelves and boxes. I motion Cassie behind me, and then shut the door as quietly and firmly as I can, trying to keep out any zombies that might have followed us. As much as I don't like having the known way out blocked, I really don't want to let any of the dead in here. As quietly as we can, Cassie and I move some of the boxes in front of the door, so any hungry empty-head will have to push very hard to get inside.

I lead the way out of the room, out through giant plastic strips hanging from the ceiling, through more storage areas, and finally to the main part of the store. I'm five steps in before I stop cold.

The lights are on.

"Delilah," Cassie whispers at my side.

"I know. Someone's here."

"No shit." She rolls her eyes.

"You said a cuss word!" I grin at her then hold my hand down low and she slaps it.

"Let's go find them," she says, and takes off running.

"Cassie," I hiss. "No! They could be dead now. They could be zombies."

But does she listen? No! She runs through the store, her sneakers slapping on the linoleum so loudly I'm sure the zombies outside can hear her.

As I race after her, I notice the sports section to my left. I take a quick detour, thinking that since I'm bigger and faster I can surely catch up. I race down one aisle full of hockey gear, do a quick turn and then thankfully reach the baseball aisle. I grab a nice aluminum bat, enjoying the feel of it in my hand. Then I cock my head to the side and try to figure out which way she's running. It sounds like she's headed to the left, to the far side of the store, so I take off in that direction.

When I catch up to her we're in the grocery section, and it reeks to high heaven. Fortunately, she's slowed down.

I shake my bat at her. "Don't do that again. For God's sake, at least walk next time if you can't wait for me."

"What's that stench?"

"I'm guessing rotting food. Definitely rotten vegetables and fruit. Probably the fresh meats, as well." I don't mention what else it could be. It could be a bunch of the good kind of dead, possibly massacred on the day everything hit, or it could be zombies. If it's the latter then we're totally screwed.

This amount of decay means there would be more of them stuck in here than the numbers out in the parking lot.

Cassie makes a gagging sound but thankfully doesn't throw up. She quickens her pace a bit, hitting the frozen food section a few steps ahead of me, and then stops in her tracks. Her mouth falls open.

I follow her eyes and almost walk into her out of surprise.

About halfway down the aisle, a grown-up is sitting on the floor; a living, breathing, human adult surrounded by food.

Chapter 32

The adult I see is not the savior I expected. I admit I figured it would be a dusty stranger with a gun slung over one shoulder and a tough but kind attitude. A grown-up who would grin and take on the responsibilities of a teenager and a child in stride. Then I could relax.

But the woman sitting in the middle of the aisle doesn't have a gun in sight. She's wearing white capris, a pink shirt and strappy white high-heels. She's also collected some of my favorite junk food, like chocolate cupcakes, nacho chips, cake, and an entire assortment of candy bars. As I'm watching, she tucks her long, blonde hair behind one ear, holds a cell phone onto her shoulder with her head, and tugs open a box of donuts.

"Hmmm – hmmm, I know what you're sayin', Crystal."

The meaning of her words hit me like a bucket of

ice water. "Delilah, is she really talking to someone on the other end of the phone?" Cassie whispers.

"No," I whisper back just as the woman notices us.

"Hold on, Crystal," she says into the phone. "You two girls go on and find your momma." She waves a hand at us then goes back to talking and eating.

I walk away from the aisle, stunned.

"How do you think she got in here unhurt?" Cassie asks.

"I don't know." I shake my head.

The one adult we've found, in all this time, is bug nuts. What the hell? Did all the good ones die, protecting me and others like me? Crap!

I suddenly feel a lot less sure about adults.

Chapter 33

We walk deeper into the store, leaving the junk food diva behind. I don't know about Cassie, but I'm still hungry even after seeing that woman on a binge. The frozen food is not an option and the fresh produce died long ago. I would really love a peach, a nice, juicy ripe one I could eat over the sink like old times. I sigh.

"Hey." I turn to Cassie. "If the lights are on, then I bet this place has an employee break room with a microwave just like the department store. We can have hot food."

Cassie grins. "Meet you there?"

"Sure. Thanks to crazy lady, I don't think there are any zombies in here – otherwise she'd be long dead – but still be safe, okay?"

She nods and runs off. I walk down the aisles, collecting canned food, microwave meals and stuff to cook them in. I also grab soda, napkins, and forks, so we can eat like civilized people.

It turns out the break room is between the restrooms and an area full of little lockers. Cassie's already in there with a pile of good stuff, but nothing's in the oven yet. Hey, I might not know how to really cook yet, but I know for sure how to make something in a microwave. I pour stew into a plastic container, following it up with noodles, and that oh-so-pleasant hum fills the room.

I sit at one of the tables while Cassie plugs in her new PSP, and she gets my new phone charging, as well. Then we crack open some soda and sports drinks and drink straight from the bottles. The blue sports drink goes down smoothly, and I remember my dad saying once that if they taste good then you really need it. I go through twenty ounces in under five minutes; I must have really needed it. I sit back and enjoy the air conditioning blasting down on us. I don't know how that woman found the power, but I sure do appreciate it. I actually feel cool for the first time in hours.

The microwave dings and I put the stew into two bowls, stopping only long enough to take a good, long sniff. *Ahhh...* Then I drain the water from the noodles, split that into two bowls, and pour a can of tomato sauce over both to make good, quick spaghetti. I place one of each in front of Cassie and then set a place for myself.

"Delilah, what's wrong with that lady?" Cassie asks while we eat.

I shake my head. "She's cracked. She can't handle it."

"Then how did she get here?"

"I'm guessing she has periods of reality, and then the rest of the time she's gone."

"Why the bad food?"

"You've never been around people who have been dieting, have you?"

Cassie shakes her head. "My family's naturally thin."

"Be glad of it. Don't ever diet. Now, here's a question for you – how do we get our stuff back without me getting eaten?"

We spend the night in the back of the SuperMart, and neither the crazy lady nor zombies disturb us. I fall asleep so stuffed my stomach hurts. When we finally settle down somewhere, those are going to be my two top priorities: AC and food.

In the morning we grab some supplies, including water bottles, some items for our attack on the zombies, and a couple of bikes. As we're about to leave, Cassie pauses.

"Should we say goodbye?"

I shake my head. "We'll just close the door good and tight. And Cassie, I know we have things to do and all, but I'd like to make a quick pit stop."

"Where?"

"The bookstore. I figure we go down the alley, I shoot the door, and we go in."

"Won't the noise alert the zombies?"

"I don't think so. She got in, after all."

"Okay." Cassie shrugs.

So we go to the door of the bookstore. Just for kicks I try the handle, but unfortunately it's locked so, looking both ways, I back up and shoot it. Thanks to my bad aim, it takes three tries but I eventually get it open. Cassie runs off to the music section – she's apparently not into books the way I am - and I just stand there a few seconds.

It's quiet, and dark, but it's just that wonderful feeling of being in a bookstore. What will I find? But, unfortunately, even though I have all the money in the world, basically, at this point I can't spend two hours in here looking for something to read.

Please, God, let us get civilization back, because I don't want to reach a point where I've read every book available.

Don't laugh – it could happen – there are only so many of them.

But this time, since I'm on a schedule, I head directly for the books I want. I go down the aisles until I find the area that has novels by Laurell K. Hamilton. I pick up a paperback, the next one in the series, the one my mom said I needed to wait until I'm older to read, and I hold it flat in my hand.

Here it is. Now I can finally know what happens next. But I just stand there and think of my mom. Before the world died, I'd been planning on reading this in spite of what she said. I was going to sneak bits of it at a time during trips to the library. And really, what can possibly be in this book that I should be protected from now, after all that's happened?

But I put it back.

"Love you, Mom," I whisper.

Then I run down the aisles to find the next book by Rachel Vincent instead. I slip it into my bag and find Cassie.

Okay, when we get set up, I'll want AC, food and a local bookstore.

#

I push open the back door to make sure our exit is clear, and unfortunately Cassie was right. The noise I made breaking into the store did bring some zombies. The good news is they're the slow kind and they're just now coming around the bend at the far end.

"Cassie, be ready to ride fast," I say and get on my bike. She pushes hers around the door, sees the empty-heads, and follows me.

I know it's stupid, but a part of me is starting to enjoy this. The day is warm, but not hot yet, and as I pedal my bike a slight breeze ruffles my hair. I imagine I look super-hot, like a young supermodel-to-be. A heartbreaker.

I glance over my shoulder and Cassie's keeping up. The zombies have reached the book shop, but won't be able to get us. This is so cool. It's like we just got away with snatching stuff from a store and the fat old cops (zombies) can't keep up.

I grin to myself and then pedal extra hard to get up the hill in front of us.

#

To be honest, even after an hour or so of riding, I really just want to pull over and read some of my new book, but I figure Cassie won't go for it. The trip back is a bit easier, thanks to pit stops where we have some of the drinks, and the bikes make it faster. I'm trying to keep my good mood going because I know what's ahead of me. I'll need to get down the hill, get our backpacks, and race back up before any of the zombies attack me.

I think about Big and Meaty grabbing my ankle so much that my skin starts to tingle there.

We stop at the edge of the crevice and get down on our tummies again to look at the situation. Big and Meaty is back in the middle of the zombie cluster. My car is still at the other end, not blown up but unfortunately still broken.

"So I make a circle around them, and try to keep them in there –"

"While I run to the car and get our packs. I'll slip mine on, run to the face, tie yours to a rope and start climbing."

"Then I'll pull up my pack."

"Sounds good."

Cassie smiles and heads over to the part of the crevice closest to the zombie circle. I put my shades on the ground and tie my shoes extra tight. I swallow some sports drink and ignore the knots in my stomach.

I stay still for a moment, trying to make everything go quiet, to block out the noise of the zombies and the heat of the sun. Then I visualize my path: down the slope, to the car, get the packs, up the slope. I envision everything going well.

I open my eyes, put the drink down, and nod at Cassie.

Chapter 34

I head down the slope, trying to run and slide as quickly as possible, while Cassie's reaching into her plastic bag and pulling out meat from the store and tossing it to the zombies. The meat's rotted, the wrong temperature, and not moving, but we're hoping it will distract them enough.

Using my peripheral vision, I can see the zombies getting excited. Unfortunately, when I'm only halfway down I notice one head swiveling my way. Of course, it's Big and Meaty. Of course, he would be more interested in moving meat than what's in front of him. I bet he was annoying in real life, too.

"Now!" I shout to Cassie. Without looking at her, I know she's reaching into her bag and pulling out a little plastic container of lighter fluid, perfect for a barbecue. As I'm racing down, trying not to fall on the rocks, she puts a circle around the zombies, lights the match and tosses it.

I'm almost at the bottom when she cries out, "It's not working!"

I stop and notice a couple of things. The matches are going out before they hit the fluid-soaked ground, and Big and Meaty is working his way out of the cluster.

"Light something like clothing and throw it down now!" I shout in a panic and take off, because I can't wait to see if it works out okay.

Out of the side of my eye I see a big white, flaming object fall to the ground and a second later, the circle catches fire.

I'm at the bottom and racing for the car just as Cassie throws something on fire at Big and Meaty, who is now definitely away from the other zombies. I jump in the vehicle and slam the door shut.

I'm in the front driver's seat. I ran a hand quickly along the dash.

"I missed you. Sorry about the accident." I know it's silly to talk to a car, but my mom did it all the time, so I'm not quite so weird.

Cassie's backpack is on the floor next to the passenger seat, so I grab that and put it next to me. Then I climb into the back and grab my pack just as something slams into the side window.

"Crap!" Big and Meaty is outside the car, his bloody hand on the window right in front of me, and he's on fire. He stares at me like I'm the cream in the middle of a cupcake, and he doesn't seem to care that he's burning.

Chapter 35

"Oh, God." I push myself as far away from him as I can, up against the far window. I'm a lousy shot, but I struggle for my gun anyway. Surely I can't miss him from this close.

"Oh, God, oh, God." I've got three bullets. I crawl back to his side, even though my heart is pounding hard, and I know, I know I don't want to get closer to him.

I sit on my knees and he stares in at me. Dear God, this is the closest I've gotten to one without it being able to bite me. His eyes are tracking me then his hand slams against the door again and I jump. But so far, he isn't figuring out to make a fist and smash the window.

How long will the glass hold?

I sit back on my haunches and raise the gun, pointing it right at his face. Only a small barrier separates us, and I see no knowledge in his eyes that

I'm basically holding a gun to his head. He doesn't know.

This isn't right. This isn't right to just shoot something point-blank like this when it can't reach me.

But he'll eat me.

Dear God. I say a prayer for myself, and for him, and for my soul, and then I turn my head away and pull the trigger.

Chapter 36

The glass explodes and I shoot until I'm out of bullets. Then I quickly scooch back on the seat and shake myself a little.

Big and Meaty is gone.

I scramble forward and look over the side of the window.

He's face-down on the ground, still on fire, and he's not moving. It reminds me a bit of how I found Cassie's dad. I think I actually shot him in the head.

I sink back into the car seat. I think he's down for the count.

Not wanting to think about anything, I shove the gun into my pack and throw the whole thing over the front seat. I climb up front, slip my pack on, grab Cassie's bag and then I'm out the door.

I step on the ground outside of the car, making sure Big and Meaty can't reach me - just in case - and I'm surprised at what I see.

The empty-heads didn't stay inside the circle.

I'm not sure why; maybe they saw what Big and Meaty was doing and decided to follow. They weren't as strong as he was, though, and the resulting smell is horrible. As I look around, it feels like my brain isn't working right. I know there are zombies in various states of burning around me; all of them on the ground and some of them still crawling. I know this, but I don't really see all of it. It's like my eyes bounce right over it.

It hits me that the fire thing had been a really bad idea.

Then I'm moving, ignoring the sick feeling in my stomach and neatly avoiding the outstretched hands of burning zombies. I know they're dead, but they still look like humans, and seeing them move all around me, on fire…

I shake my head, drown everything out, and I finally reach the side of the hill. I tie Cassie's backpack on the rope and feel better for a second.

The key to everything, the fix for the world, might be in that pack.

Chapter 37

I tug on the rope, and then the world becomes just the slope, just the rocks and dirt, and the safest way to get up there without falling.

I reach the top, dirty, and sweating, and tired.

Cassie helps me over then pulls me into a hug.

#

After a short rest, we loop around the crevice and follow the road again, making pit stops here and there to drink water, hot out of the bottle. I can't help feeling a bit sad.

This isn't what my life was supposed to be like; this isn't who I am. I'm not the type of person to go around killing things. Dang, before this I had trouble smushing the bugs that got into our apartment. After a few years of this, what will I be like? Will I even survive?

God, years of this, years of this... tears are falling

down my face and I can't stop them. I slow down to slip behind Cassie so she won't see.

#

After a few hours of riding, we stop for lunch. Cassie picks out a large tree on a hill not far from the road.

"We can have a picnic." She grins at me. I smile in response but it doesn't stay long on my face as I follow her up the slope and rest my bike on the ground. I dig in my backpack for food while Cassie spreads a blanket. I place a can of Vienna sausages in front of Cassie, and another next to me. Then I open a large can of peaches and put it between us so we can share it.

I get a couple of bites of sausage in when Cassie twists away so her back is to me. She fiddles with something, and then turns around.

"Ta-da!" She holds up a makeshift necklace; a thick, black string looped through a black thumb drive. "That's for you."

"Thank you. What is it?" I ask, taking the necklace.

"It's a copy of the lab data."

"Cassie." I look at her, stunned. "I can't." I try to hand it back to her.

"No, go ahead. I've got a copy, too." She reaches under her shirt and pulls out a necklace like mine. "I just thought you should have one, too. You know, just in case…" Her eyes slide to the ground.

"Nothing's going to happen to you, Cassie," I say firmly. "I'll keep hold of this one just in case you lose yours or get separated from it again." I slip the necklace over my head.

"Okay," she agrees.

"Hey, who has matching necklaces?" I ask, twirling mine.

"We do." She grins.

I slip the necklace under my shirt, and it clinks gently against my shamrock. We dig into lunch, eating messily but heartily, and as I get full I lean back against the tree. I'm feeling better and I have Cassie to thank for it. Giving me a copy of the lab data… yeah, that was smart, but it also shows that she trusts me. She trusts me to hang onto something important; that if used right could change the world. Looking at the little black USB drive, I realize this is the first time someone's believed in me to this degree. I want to make sure I live up to that.

I'm savoring one last bite of peach when I notice a bird flying overhead.

"Hey, Cassie, what's that?"

"It's a bird," she deadpans.

I smile and shake my head. "I know it's a bird, goober, but what kind?"

She grins, shading her eyes as she tries to catch a better look. "I think a hawk, but I'm not sure."

It's the first animal I've seen in weeks. If they can survive out here, maybe we can, too.

We spend the rest of the afternoon riding without seeing any other beings, alive or dead. We are seriously in the boonies. Eventually, I realize I haven't seen any shelter for the night – not a car or a house or anything – so I search for anything that might help us as the sun begins to set.

"How about there?" I point to a large grassy hill that has three large trees at the top.

"Sure," Cassie agrees. We eat dinner in the same way we did lunch, with a blanket on the ground and food between us, watching the sunset. Then Cassie starts to stretch out on the ground. I look around and I don't see anything, but I'm still a bit nervous. I glance at the tree behind me and notice large, strong branches.

"Hey, Cassie. Just to be safe, how about we sleep in the tree?"

"Sure. That'll be neat."

She scales the tree like it's as easy as walking up her staircase at home. It takes me a bit longer, and I gain some scrapes and bruises, but eventually I get up there. I shift around a bit until I wind up facing a branch, wrapping my legs around it, and then kind of lying down. It's not very comfortable, but hopefully I won't fall this way.

"Goodnight," I call to Cassie, and notice she's

already fallen asleep. I watch the night deepen, very black with no moon, and try not to think any thoughts. I try to just empty my mind and think about the present – the bark beneath my cheek, the tree beneath me and the soft sounds of the night. Eventually, I fall asleep.

When I wake the next morning my cheek is scratched all over, but at least I'm still in the tree and so is Cassie. This turns out to be a very good thing, because sometime in the night we've attracted four zombies.

Chapter 38

They stand beneath the tree and stare at us. There's an adult male zombie, with cracked brown eyes and short brown hair that has a cowlick, who's wearing jeans and a white shirt covered in brown stains. Then there's a female zombie with long sandy-blonde hair. She wears a long, blue cotton dress covered in flowers, and she shifts from foot to foot, glancing down at the ground and then occasionally back up at us as if she keeps forgetting something. Beside the woman are two boys, both dressed in tan shorts, sandals and white t-shirts, like they skipped school to come and drool over us. The smallest one is around five years old, while the older one is maybe seven or eight. There's blood on the youngest boy's mouth, and a matching wound on the woman's neck. I think they're a family.

I search the rolling hills for where they came from. I don't think we made much noise during the night, so they had to have been nearby. I stretch upwards a bit and notice what looks like a bit of a roof far off to the left.

I look back down at the zombified nuclear family and wonder how to get down.

"Any ideas?" I ask Cassie. "I'm really not into using the gun at this point, and I can't reach them with my bat."

"I shoot them?" She grins.

"No." I shake my head. "You're not good enough with a gun yet. You might shoot me by mistake."

"Good point."

Logistically, I'm trying to figure this out. If I jump down then I can attack them with my bat, but with four of them total I'll be a goner in no time.

"What if we throw cans at them?"

"Probably not heavy enough to really do anything. But what about our backpacks?" I ask.

"Sure, but we only have two of those. Who do we aim for?"

"Both of the adults. I think I can then take out the kids."

"Delilah, we're supposed to be partners, remember?"

I stop, look up at her serious face and realize she's right. We agreed to be partners, and I could really use her help.

"You're right. And that would definitely make

things easier." I smile. "So which one do you want to take out?"

"Let's knock out the parents with the packs, then jump down and get the kids."

"Sounds like a plan."

So Cassie goes first, carefully lining up her backpack and then dropping it right on the father's head. I follow up quickly with a hit to the woman, and it doesn't get her full-on but it still drops her. They won't be down long, though, so I slide quickly – if painfully – out of the tree. I kick the smallest kid down to the ground and run around him to grab my bat. Meanwhile, Cassie's whacking the large kid with a tree branch.

I notice the dad is shifting out from under the backpack, so I hit him on the head until he falls down, and then I knock out the woman again for good measure. By that time, Cassie's gotten the small one to the point where he's just crawling on the ground, and she's back to hitting the large kid. I go behind him and hit him once with the bat and he falls to the ground.

"They're still twitching," Cassie says.

"I think they're still alive," I reply.

"Should we kill them?" she asks. And I know what she means. I know they can kill us and whoever else they come across, but I just feel uncomfortable killing off a family.

"Do you still have the rope from the crevice?"

"Yeah," Cassie says. So we tie them to the tree. As I'm tying up the smallest, he twitches a bit, almost coming awake right when my arm is near his mouth, and it occurs to me that with all my scrapes and cuts this was a really bad idea on my part.

I finish tying the rope and back off, looking at my arm.

"What is it?" she asks.

"All it takes is the blood, right? His blood getting into my bloodstream?"

Cassie pales.

Chapter 39

Cassie pulls my arm down until she can look at it. "Did you get any of his blood on you?"

"I don't think so, but God, Cassie, what if it's really small?"

I hit the ground with my butt, really freaking out. *Oh, God, am I about to turn into one of those things? Will I turn in a couple of hours? Will I turn and hurt Cassie?*

"You've got to shoot me."

"No! No!" She stomps her foot and puts her fists on her hips. "Stop it! I don't see any blood on you. He didn't get near you! Now, come on." She pulls her bike upright, climbs on and rides away slowly.

I sit there a few minutes, looking at my arm then watching the squirming zombies who've come awake and, upon seeing me, start to moan.

The smallest boy reaches a hand out to me.

I shiver, then jump up and follow Cassie.

I hope to God she's right.

I stumble through the grassy hills, my attention more focused on my arm, like I can see the virus spreading, than on the ground. Please, God, don't tell me that my weird sudden desire to keep something kind of living has resulted in my death. That would suck.

I know all the signs of the sickness coming on – it's just like the flu: sneezing, coughing, fever, chills, and occasionally throwing up. It differs from person to person as to how long it takes; anywhere from ten minutes to twenty-four hours. It's all based on your immune system and your DNA. We were just getting into genetics in school when everything went to hell.

I'm staring at myself so much I don't see a rock, and I fall heavily to the ground. Cassie notices and marches back to me, her forehead wrinkled and a stern look in her eyes.

She takes my arm and examines it thoroughly, then lightly coasts her fingers over my skin.

"There's no wetness, no indication of saliva or blood," she says, her voice sounding so grown-up I wonder if she's channeling her father. She puts a hand on my forehead. "You don't have a fever. Do you feel the urge to sneeze or cough?"

"No." I shake my head.

"Then you're fine."

"But –"

"Yes, I know it could hit later, especially because you've had The Shot. That will change how you respond to the virus. But there's nothing on your arm. You're fine. If you want to worry for a couple of hours, that's up to you."

For a moment, she reminds me a bit of my mom. Cassie turns sharply on her heel and heads to the roof I can now see quite well.

I sigh and try to slow my pounding heart with deep breaths. I'm a worrier and I know it, but it seems like this would be quite the thing to be concerned about.

Surely I would know if I was changing, right?

"Just think of something else!" Cassie shouts at me.

Something else, something else... so I follow her, doing my best to remember the entire plot of the last book I read.

Chapter 40

It doesn't take very long until we reach the house even though we're just walking and pushing bikes. It makes sense that the zombie family found us. By the time we get there, though, I'm feeling much calmer. Thankfully, Cassie's trick has worked. Well, that and I'm still not feeling any symptoms.

Okay, yes, maybe I overreacted. But wouldn't you be scared, too?

Deep breath, Delilah, I think you made it. This time.

I reach the top of the hill, and down below is a gorgeous little farm. There's a white two-story house with green trim and a front porch, a brown building that appears to be a detached garage, another white building about the size of the garage, a swing set, and a small garden near the main house. Past the white building and to the far right is a field of corn grown tall, with some of the stalks already browning. I don't know at this point if we're still in

Texas, or if we've ventured into a part of Oklahoma or Colorado yet, but I'm betting they gave up their regular crop this year to start growing corn for ethanol.

Cassie is, of course, already down the hill, but I'm surprised to see that instead of running for the house she's headed for the swing set instead. As I watch she launches herself onto one of the seats and is happily swinging back and forth as I walk down.

I drop my bike at the base of the hill and toss my backpack down after it. It's nice and cool. There are large trees all over that create a wonderful shaded area near the house and also create an illusion of a normal lawn. I slip off my shoes and socks and stand on the wonderful, soft grass. I close my eyes and take a deep breath. The scents of the grass, the trees, and nature all blend together and just smell, well, green. I just listen to the crickets chirp for a few minutes. There's a mild breeze as well, as soft against my skin as an expelled breath.

I'm a city girl at heart, but this is nice. Peaceful.

I open my eyes and wander around the property, skirting quickly past the peeling paint of the house, the garden and Cassie on the swings. I walk to the edge of lawn. There's an irrigation ditch full of water, followed by a foot of dirt, and then the field of corn. It looks peaceful, too, but anything could be back in that green maze. I wonder if it's ready yet, or if it's overripe. If I take some of the stalks, can I eventually cook it and eat it, or will it go bad on the way? I don't know.

I turn away from the crop and my gaze falls on the white building. Maybe it's a storage area? I cross the ten feet or so, find a wooden door, also painted white, turn the knob and open it. It takes a few seconds for my eyes to adjust to the darkness before I step a foot inside, noting that the floor is just dirt. There's a silence, a stillness, but it still feels like there's something wrong. Then I hear a low moan that kick-starts my heart, and I hear the soft sounds of feet shuffling. I whirl, getting outside in a second and slamming the door shut.

I lean against it and I can still hear them moving inside. One of them walks into the wood and I scream without meaning to, covering my mouth quickly with my hand to keep from doing it again. I can hear their excited moans.

I grab a stick and I'm jamming the door just as Cassie races around the corner.

"It's okay." I hold my hands up and gesture behind me. "Just don't go in there. Packed full of zombies."

"You okay?"

"Yeah, just shaken."

She grins and takes off, back to being a kid. Slowly I sink to the ground, turning to watch the building. The grass is soft and cool beneath me and a gentle breeze blows my hair, bringing with it that scent that I can't place, the one that just smells green to me. If I didn't know what was behind that door, this would be a truly peaceful place.

Then I notice the bloody handprint on the side of the building and everything snaps into place. The little boy with the red mouth must have somehow wandered into the zombie room and been attacked, and his mother, after finding this out, had let him turn her.

I can imagine her holding him to her throat with tears streaming down her face because her little boy is gone.

And I understand that love makes us do these things, but to actually do it...

My mom died for me without any hesitation. I mean no hesitation at all. That took guts. And where on Earth was her common sense, her sense of survival?

I mean, I know parents are supposed to protect you. But I think I would have paused. And I did. It was my mistake, I was frozen and my mom stepped in and saved me. It was my mistake, for God's sake!

And she just did it.

What does it take to be like that? What strength of character means that you don't even slow down on the way to your death?

Is that what it means to be somebody?

Chapter 41

After a while, I get up and explore the rest of the property. Carefully I go into the garage, expecting another zombie horde, but even with my bat raised at the ready I don't find any undead inside. Instead I find a black Jeep, complete with a hardtop and doors. Nearby, I find a few red plastic gas cans which feel full, and when I peek inside the back I can see cans of food and bottles of water.

It looks like they had the get-away vehicle all ready to go but never had the chance to use it. Now I wonder if I can find the keys. I go up to the front, open the door and find the keys dangling from the ignition. I guess when all of the neighbors are dead you can leave the keys in the car without worrying about it being stolen. Then I notice the Jeep's a stick. Crap. I don't know how to drive that. But then again, how hard could it be? I slam the door shut and then go back outside to find Cassie waiting for me.

"I thought we'd both go inside the house together," she says.

"Good idea."

I lead the way to the front door and Cassie holds the screen door open while I twist the knob. It turns easily, so I gently push the door and raise my bat. Nothing jumps out, so I step into the house and let my eyes adjust. To my left is a door which I'm pretty sure is a closet, and straight ahead is a set of stairs and then a hallway leading to the back of the house. To my right is a family room, although it probably started life a hundred years ago as a parlor. The furniture isn't like Cassie's house; instead, it's more like what I'm used to – a green couch flanked by two mismatched white, cushy chairs, all of which face a TV that's a nice size but definitely isn't a big-screen or even a flat-screen. There are two game controllers on the carpet, like they were just put down for a second, and I can see a big, yellow dump truck pushed under one of the coffee tables.

I let Cassie inside and then I lead the way down the hallway, which is mostly uneventful except for an empty bathroom on the left. I reach the end of the hall and walk into a nice-sized kitchen, complete with a round wood table, four chairs, and another door leading outside.

Cassie follows me in, flips a switch and floods the room with light.

"Ha! I thought they might have a generator." She grins.

We go through the rest of the house but don't find any zombies. After the search, we come back to the kitchen and raid the fridge.

I do feel a bit icky about it, because I know exactly where the owners are, but really they can't use it and there's no real way I can pay them back. The best I can do for them is a silent prayer that their souls will be okay. Yes, I have issues with religion, but I definitely believe we have souls.

The refrigerator contains genuine fresh tomatoes that burst with flavor as soon as I bite into one. Normally I'm not all into the whole fruit and vegetables thing, but it's been months since I've had any, much less fresh ones.

"I know we haven't gone very far today, but how about we stay here for the night?" I ask Cassie.

"Sounds good to me," Cassie replies, following it up with a bite of tomato.

It's been, well, a really long time since I've had a bath or a shower. It's odd. I used to take one without a thought every day, and now it feels like a huge luxury.

I go upstairs to the big bathroom, and thankfully I'm right; the plumbing works, including hot water from the tap. I fill the tub, including this nice lavender soap thingy I find in a dish on the counter, and then I slip into the water. Oh my gosh, I almost fall asleep. You have no idea how good this feels, to actually bathe after weeks without it. And boy, was I dirty.

After my bath, I go downstairs and find Cassie playing with her PSP, so I bring out my book and start to read. Finally, time to read ... Again, it's weird how the normal things are now luxuries.

#

The next morning the sun is shining, and there's a small breeze that makes all of the green leaves of the trees flap against each other. It is so peaceful here. I really want to stay. I raise my head to call out to Cassie, to suggest we live here and maybe build a lab in the basement, but then I stop. We began this whole thing with a search for grown-ups; it's possible that Cassie won't want to settle down until we find some who still have their act together.

I wonder about that for a moment, and then I realize a part of me doesn't think we're going to find any.

What if we will be the first adults of this new world? I grin to myself. Then it will be a lot easier to make a better world.

With a bit of energy in my step at the thought, I sling my backpack over my shoulder and go to the garage. I throw open the back hatch of the Jeep, and over a few trips I fill the back with the gas and my pack. Then I lash our bikes to the spare tire on the hatch.

And then I realize I have done all of this without Cassie's help. Where is she? At first, I'm annoyed at the realization. Then I remember what the world is like and I race out of the garage.

Chapter 42

"Cassie!" I scream. Oh, God, please don't say that while I was stupidly filling up the getaway car she got attacked by a zombie. "Cassie!"

"What?!"

I round the corner of the garage and on the other side is this huge, grassy area. Cassie's there, throwing a stick for a dog.

A dog, for God's sake. I take a deep breath, calm down, and get it back in my head that she's safe.

She's playing with a golden retriever. It's a bit dirty, but doesn't look too bad considering the state of the world. Right now the dog's picked up the stick in its mouth, its tongue lagging out around the wood, and for all the world it looks happy. It runs back to Cassie, drops the stick on her feet and sits on its haunches, wagging its tail.

She picks up the stick, throws it, and the golden retriever dashes after it.

"Isn't it wonderful?" Cassie asks with a big smile, and her whole face is lit up, almost as good as when she got her PSP.

"Yes," I agree, watching the dog. Humans are the only animals that can catch the zombie virus, so the animal's safe. The virus is almost oddly, resoundingly, stuck within the confines of humanity. Of course, that knowledge is quite a few months old; things may have changed since then. But either way, watching that retriever, I knew it was out of harm's way.

"Can we keep it?" Cassie asks.

I know we shouldn't. I can think of a thousand reasons why we shouldn't. We could get attacked and the dog could die, we could lose it, we could lose our lives trying to protect it. I can feel fear just building up in me at all of the ways we can lose the retriever. But just to see it run, to see the joy that is a dog… I'm sorry, I can't give that up.

"Definitely." I nod.

"What should we name her?" Cassie asks.

"Her?" I ask, just as the dog comes rushing up to me. She drops the stick on the grass near my feet and shakes herself with delicious anticipation. I kneel and extend my hand right below her nose; she dips her head and sniffs me, the warmth of her outgoing breath hitting my hand, and all I can smell is pure doggy goodness.

"How about Sunshine?" I say, giving her a quick pat on the head, then grabbing the stick and throwing it with all my might.

"Sunshine?"

"Yeah, you know, like that song. 'Sunshine, my only sunshine, you make me happy, when skies are gray.'" I stop when I realize Cassie's laughing at me.

"What? You don't like the musical stylings of Delilah?" I cock one hip out, put a hand on it, and give her a snobby look. She collapses into giggles and the dog runs over and starts licking her.

"Sunshine it is." She laughs.

We go to the Jeep, and Sunshine jumps into the backseat like she's used to it. Is she their dog? *Okay, enough. I'm not going to feel bad about them anymore.*

I slide in the front, Cassie sits in the passenger seat and we both slam our doors at the same time. I turn the key, get the engine going, and then stare at the dash like it can tell me something.

"What's wrong?" Cassie asks.

"I don't know how to drive a stick."

"Don't look at me." She shrugs.

There are three pedals on the floor and I know two of them, so I put one foot on the brake and another foot on the new pedal. Now, I know the stick in the middle of the car has something to do with the whole thing, so I put my hand on the black knob and I push forward. Nothing happens, so I push it backwards, and it squiggles beneath my hand. Really odd. Anyway, I futz with it, and after about ten minutes, plenty of sighs and toe-tapping on Cassie's part, we finally back out.

We leave the garage, and then through starting and stopping, jerking us all back and forth until Cassie screams, I finally figure out how to go forward.

"Got it," I say, and drive out of the yard. Sunshine leans around the seat to lick Cassie's face, making her smile and hug the dog with one arm, and I look in the rearview mirror once more back at the house. What I see almost stops me and the car.

In front of the porch is a small girl, no more than five, dressed in pajamas and holding a teddy bear while watching us. I don't see evidence of a bite, but I can see the signs of the virus in her face and in her cracked eyes.

Dear God, where did she come from? Had she been in the house with us?

She just stands there as I drive off, holding her bear.

Chapter 43

I think the freeway is behind us. I'm driving down a long, country road, and I'm hoping I'm heading toward some kind of town.

"Any idea where we are?"

"No." Cassie rolls her eyes.

"How about the freeway?"

"I think it's behind us."

"Any idea how to get there?"

"No," Cassie says and puts some of her hair in her mouth, dragging it through until it's wet while looking out the window.

"Thanks," I mumble to myself.

"I want some gum," she states, chewing on her hair. "Let's stop at the next town."

"Sure," I agree and grip the wheel. She's getting on my nerves. First she didn't help me load the car, and now she's just being annoying. She starts making this clicking sound and I try to let it go, but then I snap.

"Cassie!"

"What?"

"Stop that."

She shrugs and starts playing with her hair again. I know what's wrong. Even though we just had a nice rest period, we've been traveling for days and we've only been around each other. Whether there are adults out there or not, it would be good to just find more people, so we'll have someone else to bounce off.

In about twenty minutes, I come up a hill and see the edges of a town about a mile away.

"Okay, Cassie, get ready. We're about to get you some gum and find out where we are," I say. Cassie straightens up, spitting the hair out of her mouth.

We crest the hill and head into town, and all I can think of is 'welcome to small-town America'. We're on the main road, and I can see a few more roads running parallel on each side, but this is seriously the major street. There's a gas station to my right, in an old white-brick building that was probably built back in the 1950's, then a liquor store and a women's clothing store. We drive over some railroad tracks and then we're in the main part of town, passing a small local pharmacy, followed by a Dairy Queen on the left.

I'm getting a vague sense of creepiness, of something being a bit off, when Cassie identifies the issue for me.

"Where are the bodies? Where are the zombies?"

God, she's right, that's it. The street is clean and empty. I don't see any blood on any of the buildings, and there just aren't any corpses, moving or still.

It's just creepy.

There are still cars parked here and there, but there is no sign that anything went wrong in their world. The only oddity is that it looks like the zombies passed them by and left the whole town empty. For months now, I've been jumping inside at the movement of other beings. I've been looking for dead things out of the side of my eye, and I've been listening for moans. I have been hunted for months, and now I'm not.

What the fuck?

Where did they all go?

Chapter 44

Cassie is surprised, too, her mouth open but without any words coming out as she looks from one side of the street to the other.

"Do you see anything yet?"

"No," she says.

So I make a sweep of the entire town, driving around 25 miles an hour. There's a huge, green park in the middle of town, empty of everything except green grass, trees, a playground and sculptures. No humans anywhere. I turn left and we're on the smaller side streets, lined by older trees and small houses, some of them from the fifties and others maybe a century or older.

"Bomb shelters?"

"Maybe," I admit. "But did they all instantly give up at the first news? Shouldn't there be some blood somewhere?"

"Yeah," she says softly, as I turn and we drive

down the main strip once more.

"Let's stop at the playground."

"Why?"

"I want to play for a bit, duh," Cassie remarks.

"Cassie, I don't think that's a good idea," I counter, but I'm talking to air because she's jumped out and is running towards the gorgeous green grass, leaving the door and my mouth wide open.

Okay, that's getting really annoying. She just runs off, repeatedly, whether it's a good idea or not.

And there goes the dog out the open door, too.

I scowl, shut the door, and pull the Jeep to a parking spot. I grab my bat and slam the door, but it doesn't grab Cassie's attention. She's on the merry-go-round with Sunshine following alongside on the ground, barking.

I stand there with my bat in hand and wonder what to do. The town is empty, so we're probably all right, but it still makes me a bit nervous.

I take a deep breath, tell myself to relax for once, and drop the bat on the ground. I haven't had a good run in weeks; okay, outside of running from zombies, but that doesn't count because I was all stressed out. I haven't had a run that was for exercise that stretched my body and left me feeling good inside.

I warm up for a few minutes, and then I start to jog along the outer edges of the park. I quickly fall into that stride that feels like I could go for hours. I breathe in and out, relaxing into the motion, concentrating on just running. Eventually I hit that sweet spot where it just feels good, and I smile.

I'd been thinking about joining track next year, but I was worried that competition would ruin this, ruin this joy I feel when I run. Little did I know...

The funny thing is I've never been good at sports. I think it's partially that I don't like things coming at my head, and a lack of coordination, and I just seem to hesitate. That's what it is: hesitation. Will I act at the right time? Will I do the right thing? Other people seem to know what to do all the time: the girls playing baseball or soccer, the guy facing down the bully, my mom stepping in to protect me from zombies. I always freeze. I miss the soccer ball headed for me, because surely that's not for me, right? I mean really, should I kick it, or is someone else going to get it? And that mean guy, if he's talking to me, surely I'll get hurt if I say something back.

I come to a stop. I think I might be a coward.

I remember instances, now that I think about it, times throughout my life where I probably could have stood up, or stopped, or something. Yes, Cassie runs into every situation, but I always seem to be on the sidelines somewhere. When it was smarter to keep my mouth shut, or let someone else take the risks, I did. When people came after me, I ran. When they came after me and Mike was around, he took the hit for me. It was the same way in school; if I had friends around then they handled the problem for me.

I never acted when there were other people around who could take the action.

I never stood up for anyone, not when Tonya was in trouble, and definitely not when Mike needed help. I saw the drug use long before my parents did and I ignored it. Sure, I had the excuse of hurt feelings, that Mike stopped hanging out with me, but I never tried to get him to stop.

I blamed my parents for failing to get Mike help. I blamed all of them for our family falling apart, but I was there, too. Could I have stopped it? If I had stepped in, if I had stepped up, could I have stopped it? Could I have helped Mike?

A drop of water falls in the dirt and I kick it away with my shoe while blinking furiously. I look in Cassie's direction and all of my self-absorbed thoughts fall away, swept clean like dishes off a table at a sight I never would have expected.

There are children and teenagers scattered throughout the park, like they were coming to play and then stopped, all of them in disarray, and each of them a zombie.

Chapter 45

Dear God, what the hell?

I dash away the tears that were forming in my eyes with my hands and get a better look at the situation.

Cassie's still on the merry-go-round, but she's holding on to a metal loop and standing still, her mouth open as she circles slowly round and round.

Where is Sunshine? My heart jumps a beat and then I see her behind Cassie, safe on the swirling playground toy.

The zombies are still just standing there. There are ones near Cassie, a couple near me and the rest are at various points around the park, like a game of red-light-green-light when the light is red.

I look at the zombie nearest me, a girl close to me in age. She's dressed in jeans and a pink top, with black sneakers decorated with pink hearts. Her skin is pale white, but it looks cracked, like her skin is earth that's been dry so long it's separated into little dry islands. Her pale blue eyes stare at me, completely lacking in emotion and recognition. The girl's blonde hair hangs limply. There isn't a scratch on her. She's like some of the young zombies I've seen – the babies and toddlers – with the cracking of the skin and eyes that indicates the virus has hit, but without any bite marks or chunks missing out of her.

There's a tall boy just past her, who was maybe sixteen when this happened, and he stares at the ground, looking lost and forlorn in an old-fashioned hat from the fifties. There isn't any sign of damage on him, either; just brown, cracked skin.

I look across the park and it's all the same. None of them were attacked.

As I'm searching for a real zombie victim, a two-year-old girl near Cassie throws her head back and cries – not moans – but cries just like a little kid would. And then the rest of them do it, too.

It's just loud and creepy. That's when I notice that every single one of them is wearing an orange band.

As I watch, adults appear on the streets, next to houses, in yards. All of them are zombies, all of them are wearing the bands, and none of them show the signs of a zombie attack. They reach a certain point, stop, and then they moan; that loud, long zombie moan.

"Dear God," I say under my breath, and then yell

at Cassie to get to the Jeep. She jumps off the merry-go-round, with Sunshine following, and I run.

I thought they would reach out, would try to catch us, but none of them move. I weave through a path of the dead and I'm untouched.

I reach the Jeep panting, but I make it safely inside and start her up.

"They've quit," Cassie comments.

"Quit what?"

"The moaning."

And she's right. They've stopped moaning and they just stand still and stare at us. It's like they feel we're not right, because we're not like them.

"Cassie, is it possible they took The Shot and turned immediately?"

"I don't know. It didn't happen in trials. From what I've seen, The Shot makes people stay more human." She shrugs.

"What about a whole town doing it, at the same time?"

"I don't know. I'll have to think about it."

We drive in silence, with me slowly curving the vehicle around the zombies in the street. They still just stand there, but I don't trust it. I have the wheel in a death grip as we head out of town.

The whole thing makes me wonder. Was everybody in town related, with the same genetic base, or did they all get the same batch of The Shot?

If one batch of The Shot was contaminated, were there any others? Are there whole towns out there like this?

Chapter 46

I drive us out of there, sincerely creeped out. What's up with a bunch of zombies that don't even attack us? It doesn't make sense.

We find a gas station about two miles outside of town, so we run in to grab a map and some gum. Fortunately, there aren't any zombies in there.

As we leave, I notice someone's spray-painted the brick side of the store with a single, short message: "We're all pretty now."

I glance at Cassie but she doesn't seem to notice it.

I drive for about ten minutes to make sure we're safely away from the town and then pull the Jeep off the road. I spread the map on the hood until I realize Cassie can't see it very well, so I put it on the grass and use rocks to keep it there. She comes over, popping her gum.

"I think we're just in Colorado." I tap my finger

on the paper. "I figure if we head west we can make it back to the freeway."

Cassie examines the map by crawling onto it and wrinkling it in spots. "Delilah, are we in a hurry to get to a certain spot? I mean, get to a certain place in Colorado by a certain time?"

"No." I shake my head. "Why?"

She grins, then jumps up and runs to the Jeep. She comes back with a slightly tattered brochure in one hand, holding it out to me. I open it up and find it's an ad for a place in Colorado called Garden of the Gods, and it looks magnificent.

"I think it's here." She lands on the map and I wince. She points at a spot that doesn't look too far from the freeway.

I crawl next to her, trying to find the various points in my head. I'm horrible at reading maps, but in a few minutes I put it together.

"Yeah, I think if we go here, here and then here we can get there."

"Cool!" Cassie jumps up and down, and then twirls and jumps.

I wait until she's slightly off-balance, and then push her just a bit. She stumbles, but catches herself and then runs full-tilt at me, pushing me backwards a bit. We giggle and push each other back and forth to the car.

#

I drive for hours and hours, and we all eventually settle into a routine. Sunshine at one point crawls into Cassie's lap, and then with many protests from Cassie sticks her head out the window. Eventually, Cassie gets the large dog into the backseat and rolls up the window while I laugh at her. About four hours in, we pull over at a rest stop.

There are abandoned cars here, of course. There's a large, white vehicle – somewhere between a station wagon and an SUV – with one of the back doors open and blood on the side. There's food everywhere, although it's obvious that animals have eaten what they can. And there's a family of three at one of the picnic tables, slumped over on the table, holding hands.

I watch the family for a few moments, looking for signs of undead life. I can't see much of their faces, but I can see their hands. The man's are pale, sickly white and do appear a bit cracked. The woman has nicely manicured, bright red nails, but all of that effort was wasted. Her hands, and that of her little boy's, have no signs of cracking and no signs of the virus. So maybe the father got the virus, and they all decided to kill themselves before he died?

I don't see any signs of gunshot wounds, but it's still possible.

I drive to the very end, far away from the little family, and Cassie and Sunshine get out and play fetch. I find a nice table near a wooded area, put a blanket down, and set out a can of meat, a bag of chips, and a can of fruit. I open everything up and call Cassie over, and she sits across from me while Sunshine comes up to my side. She sits on her rump, wags her tail, and grins at me with an open mouth. It's at that point I realize we don't have any dog food.

"Okay, but don't get used to this. We'll pick you up some dog food soon." I empty out one of the cans of meat onto a paper towel and put it on the grass for her to eat.

"We need to find her some water, too."

"Good idea. Make sure she goes to the bathroom." I grin. I love to hand out chores as long as I don't have to do any. Cassie rolls her eyes at me.

We eat lunch and Cassie takes care of Sunshine while I clean up. I notice the dog ate the paper towel along with the meat, but hopefully that won't hurt her.

What's weird is that I'm kind of excited we're in Colorado. I mean, I've never done that before. I've never made a big decision like moving to another state and having it happen, not having to ask permission of anybody else – just deciding, 'hey, this is what I'm going to do' and doing it. Pretty cool. I could get used to this.

I wonder what other things I will get to decide.

Like what our house will look like, how the lab will be, where we'll wind up?

I grin and get into the Jeep.

#

I think we're about two hours away from the Garden of the Gods. I've done my best to stay away from the towns, even though we've had some very boring scenery. I crest a hill, notice a nice grassy area to the side and pull off onto it. We all get out of the Jeep for a good stretch and I walk to the end of the lawn while drinking from a water bottle.

It turns out to be the edge of a cliff, not so high that I feel nervous but enough to give me a beautiful view of the land below. It is more grassland, with a few rolling hills and one or two trees. There's also a black truck with four doors and a horse trailer attached to the back.

"People. Look, Delilah, adults!" Cassie points, and now I see them, too. It looks like three adults in all, and a young boy, all near one of the trees.

"Cassie, wait!" I say, but I really should give up on that, because she never listens anyways. She and Sunshine are already part-way down the side of the cliff, following a tiny path.

I look at the group, and I can't say why I'm nervous, but my heart is pounding. Something about the whole group doesn't feel right.

Chapter 47

I'm probably just nervous about meeting a new group. Geez, a while ago I thought the best thing for Cassie and me would be to have some other people around and now I want to hold back. I shrug, close up the Jeep, and follow her down.

Maybe one of these days, instead of holding back, I'll race down ahead of her.

By the time I reach the bottom of the hill, Cassie is already talking with the group. I figure, damage done, so I slow down and just walk up to them.

There are three adult males: one in his twenties, another in his thirties, and the last in the eighties somewhere. There's also a young boy around Cassie's age. If we join them, then the group will be outnumbered with people who need help, instead of caretakers.

"And this is Delilah." Cassie gestures toward me with a big smile. I smile as well, and take the hand of the adult nearest me.

"I'm Jim." His hand grips mine in a nice, firm shake and his brown eyes look steadily into mine. He's wearing a plaid shirt that's open at the front, with a brown t-shirt beneath it, along with blue jeans and sneakers. His hands are dirty and he smells a bit, but then don't we all.

"Nice to meet you." I end the handshake.

"This is Todd." Jim gestures to the younger adult male. Todd's wearing a yellow polo shirt, blue jeans and tan shoes that don't look great to run in. He has sandy-blonde hair and green eyes. I take Todd's outstretched hand and he proceeds to try and crush my bones. I don't know what to do, so I just squeeze back as hard as I can and meet his gaze. His eyes burn into me, like if he looks hard enough he'll find the answer to a question. I don't like touching him.

I end the handshake and drop my hand against my pants, trying not to rub it against the material.

"This here's Grandpa and Roman." Jim gestures at the old man and little boy. "Grandpa really isn't grandpa; he just can't speak so we don't know his real name."

"Oh," I say.

Grandpa's wrapped in a blue blanket and sits on the ground as if he's really tired. Roman clutches the old man's hand. He watches me while he reaches out and slowly pets Sunshine, his movements tentative and his manner skittish. He has dark brown hair, brown eyes, and wears shorts, a t-shirt and very dirty sneakers.

"We were just about to start a fire and make dinner. Care to join us?" Jim asks.

"Yes," Cassie answers quickly.

"Yes, thank you," I say. "But won't the fire draw zombies?"

"The stiffs? Nah, we got some protection against them."

Cassie cocks her head, and since I can't see a weapon on the man, I'm curious, as well.

"Go ahead and show them, Todd." Jim grins.

Todd walks to the horse trailer, nice and slow. He pulls some gray work gloves out of his back pocket and puts them on. Then in one neat motion he opens the trailer doors, grabs a rope and yanks.

Two zombies fall out of the back of the trailer.

Chapter 48

Todd laughs then pulls them to their feet using the rope as leverage. He throws the end of it into the trailer and slams the doors shut with his foot, essentially anchoring them. I wonder if it will hold.

One of them is a man who's almost six feet tall and has a big, round beer belly. He's wearing a white button-down shirt, blue pants that were nice at one point and brown dress shoes. I don't think he made it far into the attacks. There are chunks missing from his neck, hands, and thighs. He has a big round face, with the cracked skin of the virus, and two small, cracked brown eyes. There's duct tape on his mouth.

The other zombie is taller, maybe six-foot-two to six-foot-five, and he's wearing a blue button-down shirt with black pants. I wonder if the two worked together and got attacked at the same time. He's more together than Beer Belly, at least I think so until I notice a huge portion of his skull is gone, revealing a bit of his brain. He won't last long with it exposed like that. Unlike his companion, he's African American, so the signs of the virus are harder to see from a distance. I can still see a bit of the cracked skin, though. He has duct tape on his mouth, as well.

"How are they protection?" Cassie asks.

"They're not real loud thanks to the tape, but if they know stiffs are nearby then they moan and vibrate back and forth."

"How do they know if zombies are nearby?"

Jim shrugs. "Beats me. I don't know if they have great hearing, or if they just know, somehow. But they always do. As far as we can tell, the moaning starts about five miles out, and the wobbling starts at two."

"As far as you can tell?" I ask.

"We've done a bit of testing." His eyes slide away.

"Now, how about dinner?" Todd changes the subject.

"Sure." Cassie smiles.

We gather some sticks and then the guys get the fire going. I reach into my backpack and pull out some carrots we got from the farm house. I was saving them for later, but I figure if they're going to feed us that it would only be polite to share. I put down a blanket near the fire and put the carrots on top.

"Be careful with that blanket, girl." Todd nods to the fire.

"I was." I bristle. I don't like him telling me what to do. Cassie shoots me a look, so I don't say anything more.

Todd grabs some of the sticks that didn't make it into the fire, reaches into a cooler and brings out a piece of steak then pushes it onto the stick. He hands it to Cassie and then proceeds to make three more, passing one to Jim and one to me.

"What about them?" I gesture to Roman and Grandpa.

"Oh, they're vegetarians," Todd says, and giggles. The sound goes right up my spine, like greasy fingers along my skin.

I grab all but two of the carrots and I hand them to Roman. He smiles really big, handing some of them to Grandpa and then crunching into one right away.

"I haven't seen fresh vegetables in a while," Jim says.

"Yeah, we got lucky a while back. I haven't seen fresh steak in ages, either," I respond.

"Yeah, we got lucky, too." Jim replies. The two men hold their kabobs over the fire and Cassie follows their example. I hold the stick up in front of my face, twirling it and looking at the meat. It looks okay. It looks fresh and it doesn't look like it's had maggots on it or anything. I go ahead and thrust my stick near the fire.

It takes forever to cook, and it leaves me really wishing for a microwave. While I'm waiting, I go ahead and open a couple of cans of peaches and hand them out, seeing as the majority of the carrots went to Grandpa and Roman. It looks like Grandpa's fallen asleep, but the little boy just sits there, his eyes flicking from me, to Todd and Jim, and finally to the zombies. Both of the empty-heads are silent, but it still creeps me out that they're there. Why aren't they moaning at the sight of us? Are they from that town, or has Todd somehow taught them not to make noise unless it's other dead? Are they tame?

Eventually the meat looks like it's finished and I take the stick away from the fire. I notice that Todd and Jim are already eating and Cassie's at about the same point I am.

I try to take a bite straight from the stick but it's too hot, so I pull a bit off with slightly burned fingers and shove it into my mouth.

"So, where are you from?" Cassie asks.

"I'm from Oklahoma City and Todd's from the Springs." Jim gestures to his friend with greasy fingers.

"The Springs?" she repeats.

"Yeah, Colorado Springs," Todd answers.

"How about you girls?" Jim smiles.

I make a big show of chewing, holding up my stick so Cassie can answer. There's something wrong with the meat. It tastes a bit off. Maybe it's already started to rot?

"So, you two have been traveling all alone?"

I see Cassie nod, and I take another bite. The texture just doesn't seem right. I root around in my backpack for a paper towel, and make like I'm wiping my mouth while I spit the piece of meat into it.

"That's just amazing. For two girls to have made it this far by yourself, you must have been really scared. We understand that you must have done just about anything to survive. A lot of tough things. Good job."

I try not to look guilty – even though I feel it – while I bury the meat in the ashes near me. Jim raises a beer to us and Todd does the same. Where did they get that? No one else is drinking anything.

"Good job, girls." Todd grins at both of us and takes a swig. It's at that point that I realize all of the food has been eaten.

I glance at Cassie, and she subtly points to a little earth mound near her. I don't think she liked it either, but neither of us wants to offend the guys.

Jim comes around the fire and sits between us, almost right on top of the meat grave. "I'm sorry, girls. That had to be awful. But you're safe with us now, right?"

"Right." Cassie smiles. Todd gets up and sits on the other side of her.

I don't like how close Jim is sitting so I try to subtly scooch away. My pulse is up and I just feel something's wrong. The way Todd's looking at Cassie; where have I seen that before?

Jim turns to me. "You're real pretty. How old are you?"

"Thanks." I try to smile, but my heart is pounding so hard I'm sure he can hear it. This is so wrong. I know it's wrong. I should do something.

Does Cassie know something's off?

I should do something, but what?

I notice movement out of the side of my eye. The zombies in the back, they're not moaning, but they're shifting. Are they wobbling?

Jim touches my knee. "Thank you for sharing the peaches with us. That was very nice of you."

I try not to squirm under his touch. Surely if I'm nice, he'll stop, right?

Cassie bolts to her feet. "I feel sick," she tells us before she walks away from the group to a tree nearby.

"I better see if she's okay," I say, glad for the excuse to get away from Jim. I walk to Cassie and whisper, "What's wrong?"

"My stomach's queasy."

"Did you eat that meat?"

"Just one bite. It seemed … off."

"Yeah, it seemed wrong to me, too," I say.

Cassie turns. "Hey, what was wrong with that meat? I'm feeling sick," she asks in a loud voice.

"What was wrong with it?" Todd giggles again.

God, men should not giggle. It's just wrong.

"Why, nothing was wrong with it." He grabs the cooler, walks over to us, and opens it so we can look inside.

Oh, God, oh, God... *that's* what was wrong with it. There's part of a person left in there.

I turn around immediately and throw up. Todd giggles again and I fall to my knees, upchucking until there's nothing left.

"Zombie or human?" Cassie asks in this cold, clear, logical voice that should never come out of a child.

Dear God, please no.

"Human," Jim answers, like he's telling us about the weather. He kneels in front of me, his eyes burning into mine. "How else would we get fresh meat?"

"I didn't eat any of it," I say, as if that matters.

"You're vegetarian, too, hunh?" He smiles and tucks my hair behind my ear with one finger. "That's okay. You're a real pretty girl."

My stomach twists, and I realize where I've seen that look before – from guys leering at me and my friends out of a van.

"Let go!" Cassie shouts. Todd's holding her arm,

so she hits him with her fist and he just laughs.

I know I have to act. Please, God, let me act.

I fall backward, away from Jim. I look over my shoulder, and the zombies are definitely wobbling now.

My hands are shaking and I feel like I have acid in my veins.

There's one thing I can think of to do. I open my mouth and I moan; a good loud, long zombie moan. Everyone stops dead still, staring at me with surprise. The two empty-heads join me, the sounds muffled by the tape on their mouths.

"You stupid bitch!" Jim yells. He comes for me, hands outstretched, face twisted with anger.

Chapter 49

I only know one defense move and I'm clumsy as hell, so I wait for him to get close then thrust my foot with all of my strength into his privates.

Jim screams and falls to the ground.

I race to the other side of the camp and grab my bat. By the time I get back, Todd has lifted Cassie off the ground and is using my best friend as a shield. *God, I felt this coming. Why didn't I do something?*

"Don't even try it." He backs away as she struggles. I grip my bat. I have horrible aim; if I try to hit him, I will hit Cassie. Then I notice he's not too far from the zombies. I try to keep the knowledge off my face and walk forward, forcing him backwards.

"Let her go." I know we only have a little time until Jim gets to his feet.

"Oh, no, little bitch. She's going to be my next steak." His eyes are half-crazed and I wonder how he ever looked normal to me.

"No, I think this time *you're* the steak." I rush in and push him back. Beer Belly takes him just as I grab Cassie. Todd doesn't scream or anything; he just tries to hang onto her. She reaches up and tears the tape off the zombie's mouth. I hold my breath, hoping the empty-head won't bite her, when she punches Todd in the stomach. It's a light blow, but he lets her go and she stumbles into my arms as Beer Belly bites him.

And then he screams.

A hand grips my shoulder and forces me around. I lose hold of Cassie, but I keep the grip on my bat. Jim punches me and my face explodes with pain. I drop to the ground. He kicks me, but I had a brother who could kick, too, and I roll away as fast as I can. I get to my feet with the bat, ready to swing.

That's when we hear it: moans. Loud, long zombie moans, and a lot of them.

"Fuck this, and fuck you." Jim runs to the truck.

I skirt around the fire and find Cassie untying Grandpa. Without us even realizing it, he'd been tied up the whole time under the blanket.

"You guys get out of here as quick as you can," I say. Roman nods, his eyes large and haunted. He leads Grandpa into the darkness.

That leaves Cassie, Sunshine and me. I think I kind of know where the cliff that leads to our Jeep is, I just don't know where the zombies are located. I do know they're coming, though.

"Take my hand. Don't let go for anything," I tell Cassie. She nods, her hand gripping mine. We head into the darkness.

#

I'm running, I can't see anything, and I'm holding onto Cassie's hand like it's a lifeline. We're surrounded, I know it. I can hear the moans all around me, coming out of the darkness. God, how many did I call?

It's pitch-black, so dark I can't see anything, and my eyes ache from trying. But my ears, oh, they work. I hear every shuffle of a zombie's footsteps, every moan, and my skin crawls at the thought of something coming out of the blackness to touch me.

I run faster and faster and my hand becomes slick with sweat.

Cassie's hand slips out of mine.

Chapter 50

"Cassie!" I scream. "Cassie!"

I stop immediately but I can't see her. I can't hear her. I'm surrounded by the dark and I'm alone.

My breath comes fast and hard, and I will my eyes to see, to just work. I'm alone. I'm by myself and surrounded by a bunch of zombies that are trying to find me and tear me apart.

I can feel the sweat cooling on my back, on the hand that so failed me. *God, where is she? Is she okay? Is she already eaten?*

I start to cry. God, I didn't want this, to die abandoned and alone, eaten alive by things that will never know what they destroyed. I don't want to die!

I can hear them. I can feel them moaning and moving, trying to find me.

I'm sweating again, my heart pulsing in my ears. I feel like I have acid in my blood, and I realize I have to run; I have to pick a direction and run, no matter what.

So I pick the way I think is right and I run full-speed.

Right into a zombie.

Just by reflex, it reaches out and its arms come around me. I scream and go wild, struggling with all my might until I slip out of its slimy grasp. I pick a slightly different bearing, put out my hands in front of me and run.

I'm racing blindly forward. *I have to live. Please, God, let me live.* I know tears are falling down my face, but I can't see, so I just ignore them.

I stop, a cramp in my side making every breath hurt. Then I feel something on the back of my neck, an exhalation and a stench so rotten I gag. I scream. I scream good and loud, and I hope the last people alive can hear me.

Something grabs my wrist and I pull back, terrified, bumping into the empty-head behind me.

"Delilah, it's me. Now run!"

Thank God, it's Cassie holding my wrist. She pulls on me and I run. I trust her completely, matching her pace and trying not to sweat, trying to keep that contact.

I'm crying, and I keep saying, "Thank you."

We slow down going up the hill, and then she puts my hand on the door handle of the Jeep while she goes around to the other side.

I yank the door open, vault inside, and slam it

behind me. Cassie closes hers just as I notice that Sunshine's in the back. Then I collapse, shaking, against the wheel.

Chapter 51

She saved me. She came back, and she saved me.

#

Cassie points me in a direction and gets me driving again. I'm still shaking a bit, but after about twenty minutes that goes away and we look for a place to hide for the night. Nothing seems safe to me, everything seems suspect, but she's right – I can't drive all night. I take the Jeep off the road and onto some grass, then up a small hill and down into a valley where we're surrounded by deciduous trees.

We lock the doors and settle down for the evening.

I try to go to sleep, really I do, but every time I close my eyes and see the darkness behind them, I feel like I'm back in the middle of that field. I keep jerking awake, and Cassie starts giving me dark looks after a while. So I keep my eyes open and stare off into the night, thinking.

She came back for me, helped me.

She didn't leave me all alone.

#

My mom always seemed strong and happy. Even after Dad and Mike left, she kept a pleasant face and tried to cheer me up. I didn't respond as well. I was angry and hurt, and I didn't want to be home anymore. Even when we moved out of our house and into the crappy apartment, I just didn't want to be there. I kept looking for Mike around every corner. So I stayed out. I stayed over at Tonya's, or I just came home late and flopped into bed. I didn't care about doing my homework anymore; instead, I scribbled something on the bus ride into school. I just hurt.

I saw my mom stumble the day she got the divorce papers. I actually came home that day – I think I had a fight with Tonya because she wanted to go out with her boyfriend that night instead of letting me sleep over – so I came home in a foul mood. Mom made spaghetti and I sat at the table, made a face and complained. She just started crying. She said something about how nothing was ever good enough for anybody, dropped her fork, went into her bedroom and slammed the door.

I just sat there, surprised.

I waited a few minutes, and then the only thing I could think to do was knock on her door. She didn't answer, though. I didn't know what to do, so I figured screw it and I went in.

My mom was on the bed, crying.

"I'm sorry, Mom," I apologized, not even really sure what I did.

"It's okay, honey. Go finish your dinner. I'm just not feeling well," Mom said.

I ignored that and walked around to the left side of the bed, sitting down near her. That's when I noticed the papers, speckled with colored plastic tabs, sitting on top of a yellow envelope. I looked closer and noticed the word "divorce". Her wedding ring was on the table next to them.

"Oh, Mom, I'm so sorry." I rubbed her back, and then she sat up and opened her arms for a hug. I hugged her, and she just held on for dear life, crying and crying with those awful sounds. I realized that she still loved Dad.

I didn't know what to say. I didn't know how to make this better, so I just stayed there and hugged her, even when it got really icky and wet. It hit me then that all those nights I'd been out, all those times I'd run away, she'd been alone.

Alone and hurt.

All those times she'd smiled and let me go out –

how many times had she been at home crying?

Tears welled up in my eyes, and it was at that point that I vowed I would come home for dinner every night, that I'd only stay out one weekend night a week, that I'd make sure my mom wasn't alone.

Being alone is one of the worst things in the world.

Chapter 52

I wake up because Sunshine is sitting in my lap and licking my face. She's heavy, and her paws dig into my thighs.

"Get off," I whisper. She whines softly and turns her head toward Cassie. Cassie's asleep, but her face is scrunched up and she's moaning "No" over and over again. I rub the dog's fur, wondering whether I should wake her up, when suddenly she screams loud and long then jolts awake.

"Are you okay?" I ask her. Her fear-filled eyes just stare at me for a few moments and then she shakes her head.

"They were coming after me."

"The zombies?"

"No. The… the… bad men." Her fists clench and she turns away from me. She looks about five years old and scared. I want to give her a glass of water and leave the light on all night. When she turns back, she's crying.

"Why were they like that, Delilah? Why did they eat people? Why did they feed me people?" She cries louder, with small, awful sounds. I gently touch her arm.

"Why couldn't they be good? Why couldn't they just be good and nice and take care of us?" Her voice is loud and ragged. She's almost shouting, and the pleading in her eyes tears into my heart like dull scissors.

"Why are none of them right? Why are none of them okay?" She screams the words, tears pouring down her face. Sunshine crawls into her lap, whines softly and starts poking Cassie with a cold nose. Cassie grabs on to the dog and cries into her fur. I reach over and hug her as best as I can.

"It'll be okay, Cassie. We'll find some good ones." I'm not sure if I'm telling the truth, and I don't know if I want to find any more adults at this point. After tonight, I think they might all be screwed up. I don't tell her any of that, though. I just let her cry, let her get it out, and hug her until she calms down.

We have to find something better soon, for both of our sakes.

#

In the morning, I let Cassie navigate to help get her mind off things. We take back roads and eat lunch in the car, stepping outside only for bathroom trips and a quick, anxious run for Sunshine. As I watch her, I keep seeing zombies pop up out of nowhere to grab my dog, but fortunately this is all in my head. I just don't feel safe right now. Well, okay, not like I felt before.

A bit after lunch we top a small hill, and about fifty feet past that is a downed helicopter. It's on one side and appears broken in the middle, like somebody took a toy version and tried to snap it in half, then just threw it down on the road when it wouldn't cooperate. It's burned in spots and looks heavier than news 'copters, so I'm pretty sure it's military. I avoid looking in the cockpit.

The Jeep rolls to a stop and I just stare at the wreck for a while. No more military, no more police, just monsters roaming the world. No more adults.

I grip the wheel then force myself to relax my fingers. I guide us around the helicopter slowly so I'll miss the damage from any debris. Cassie and Sunshine are quiet beside me.

We're about five minutes past the helicopter when Cassie points upwards, out through the top of the windshield.

"What's that?" she asks.

I stop the Jeep and peer up. At first I don't see anything, but then I see something white, dipping and then soaring upwards in the sky.

"That's not a bird." I get out of the Jeep, bat in

hand. I look up as the thing dives, watching as it slows down then circles closer to me.

I think it's a friggin' military drone.

Chapter 53

The white machine dips lower and does another circle near me, moves forward about fifty feet, and then does another lazy loop.

I think it wants me to follow it. Okay, that's it, I'm bonkers.

I get back in the Jeep and start her up.

"What are you doing?"

"I think that's a military drone, which means there is someone operating it."

"Delilah, I'm not sure about this." She looks a bit ill. I reach out with my hand and she grabs it.

"If it's a drone, then they're watching through video, and it will take them a while to come to us. We'll be really careful this time. We'll look for any signs that this person is off."

"You promise me we'll be okay?"

"I promise." I squeeze her hand and drive the Jeep forward, trying not to think about the phenomenally stupid pledge I just made.

We drive for maybe another fifteen minutes, with me feeling like a complete idiot for driving twenty miles an hour while following a flying white machine. *Yep, I'm stupid. This is going to take us right into a nest of zombies, I know it.*

I drive up another hill, and the flier dips low and lands in front of a red Jeep about one hundred yards from us. *Jeep: the vehicle of the future. Who knew?*

The door opens slowly, and a guy gets out and just stands there. Maybe we're not the only cautious ones now? Is that a good sign?

I squeeze Cassie's hand one more time and let go.

"Leave Sunshine in the car."

"But she could help us," Cassie whines.

Sunshine pants at me, tongue lolling, and I just can't do it. I can't risk her. I can't take the chance that he'll hurt her while we run, not when I can prevent it. Both of us can get back to the Jeep faster.

"No, let's keep her inside. Be sure to bring a weapon."

"That's not very friendly."

"I'm done with friendly," I state, and grab my bat. I get out, leaving the door open, and I walk a little less than halfway there then stop. I point the bat tip down, but I make sure to keep a firm grip. Cassie comes up behind me and grabs my other hand.

He leaves his car door open too and walks to us. I

can't see any weapons on his part, but I'm going to plan on him having some. I like how he's walking toward us, nice, slow and cautious.

Then I can make him out clearly. *Oh, dear God, he's hot.*

He's maybe a couple of years older than me, and taller of course. He has dyed black hair – that matte-black kind from a bottle - that's a bit spiky, a nice jaw, and these gorgeous green eyes that remind me of emeralds. He's pale and skinny; just the way I like guys. He has a bit of a vulnerable, scrappy look to him. I bet he was never popular; instead, he was one of those guys on the fringe, just a bit rougher and tougher than everyone else.

He's wearing black military boots, jeans, a black t-shirt, and one of those large, green military jackets. I bet he's hiding the weapons under that jacket.

He stops near us and I can see a bit of stubble along his jaw line.

My pulse is racing. Cassie looks at me oddly and drops her hand.

"Hi," I manage.

Please don't let him be crazy.

Chapter 54

"Hi," he replies. The tiniest hint of a smile touches his face.

"I'm Delilah, and this is Cassie." I gesture with the bat and Cassie looks at me like I've dropped off the moon.

He inclines his head. "I'm Sam."

"You all alone?" Cassie asks.

He looks at us for a moment, sizing us up, then nods. "Just me."

"Where'd you get the drone?" I question.

The bit of a smile grows into a genuine one. "There's a military base up the way."

"A military base, huh?" I repeat, while Cassie avoids my eyes. "Are we near the Garden of the Gods?"

"Yeah, I think it's about thirty minutes that way."

I look point-blank at Cassie.

"I must have taken a wrong turn somewhere." She shrugs.

"So, how long you two been traveling together?"

"A while." My bold Cassie has grown cautious.

"Where'd you start out at?"

"Where did you?" Cassie counters.

The smile disappears and one of his eyebrows rises at her question. "I started out in Denver. It didn't take me too long to get down here, but by the time I did all of the military were gone."

"Why'd you come here?" I ask.

"I figured the base would have a lot of weapons and would be better fortified than a lot of places."

"Then why didn't the military stay?" Cassie inquires.

"To protect us," he says softly. We fall quiet for a few moments then Sam breaks the silence. "Hey, would you girls like to have lunch? Maybe see the base?"

I know he doesn't know what we've just been through, but being offered food again makes me a bit nervous. Cassie motions me over and I hold up one finger to Sam. "Hang on a sec."

"If we don't eat, are you okay with this? I think he's a nice guy," I whisper.

She frowns. "I'm not sure, Delilah. What if he's all weird?"

"I'm sure he's weird. I don't think he's dangerous, though."

"Yeah?"

"Yeah. And besides, there's two of us and only one of him. I think we can beat him."

"Yeah, you and me, right?" She smiles.

"Definitely." I smile back then say to Sam, "We'll follow you in the Jeep."

"Okay," he answers.

Ten minutes later, he pulls over onto some grass at the top of a hill. I get out of the Jeep, and this time I let Sunshine out, too. He seems nice enough that I think it's safe to let her out. She jumps out of the car and shakes herself all over. Then I notice that Sam's out of his car and he's looking at Sunshine like I've seen some women look at babies – like an amazing blessing they never expected.

"May I?" he asks.

"Sure." I shrug.

He slowly approaches Sunshine and then puts his hand out near her. She sniffs him then licks his fingers, and a big smile breaks over his face. He kneels in front of her and pets her. She bumps into him and he hugs her, burying his face in her fur.

Cassie and I share a smile, and she gives me a small nod. Sunshine had stayed far away from the adults last night, so seeing her approval of Sam makes us both feel better.

He stands up and starts massaging Sunshine's back. "It's been so long since I've seen a dog, much less been able to pet one. Thank you."

"You're welcome. Sunshine's a sweetie." I pet her head.

"Sunshine, huh? Such a pretty name for such a good dog," he says, but he's talking to the dog, not me.

"Whatchya doin'?" Cassie asks.

"I'm massaging her back, following the spine. Dogs' backs can hurt just like ours, so a massage feels good to them, too."

"Oh, cool," she says, and joins in. Sam shows her how to rub Sunshine's back and steps away.

"I'll show you the base."

I follow him to the top of the hill and we look out across a valley. It doesn't look like a base. At the south end there's a cluster of buildings, then a grassy area, then more buildings. The whole section is surrounded by parking lots. The north end looks like former soccer and baseball fields, and is covered with military vehicles, including tanks and Humvee. I can't see that well, but I think the whole area's fenced in, because there's a bit of a gap and then the entire complex is ringed by zombies.

"Where's the base, exactly?" I ask.

"It's down there. This whole area was originally an Air Force Academy before the virus, and once things started to hit the fan they set up the fence and started using it as an outpost. The actual base part is there –" he points –"under the fields. I'm not sure how long ago it was built, but there's a whole area underground that was set up to be headquarters in case of an emergency."

"Oh my God. Are you saying there are still some of our military left?" Then I remember he'd already said there weren't any more.

"No," he says quietly. "Or at least not here. I'm not sure what happened, but it doesn't even look like it was used."

My hope didn't last long, but I still feel an ache in my chest. I examine the whole area and another question hits me.

"I can't help but notice there's a huge number of zombies down there. How do you plan on getting back in? Then again, how did you get out in the first place?"

Sam grins. "There's an entrance hidden in the hills behind us. The zombies haven't even come close to finding it."

"That's why you have the drone, isn't it? To check and see where you can go?"

"Exactly." He smiles. "It also helps me see where they are in the larger area, and keep a look out for regular people."

"Cool."

"I can show you, if you'd like."

"That'd be great," I agree, and then frown. "Why are you being so nice?"

"Really?" he asks. I nod to show him I'm serious. He shoves his hands in his jeans, checking to make sure Cassie isn't listening. "I haven't been around people in a while. My friend –" he pauses – "didn't make it. We had the whole thing planned, and he still didn't make it."

"I'm sorry," I say quietly.

He nods, looking at the ground. "I'd just like to be around people again."

"Even a couple of girls, huh?" I tease.

A gentle smile spreads across his face. "Yeah."

It's only after I'm back in the Jeep that I think about something. How does a kid just a couple of years older than me know about a secret military installation?

Chapter 55

We reach the entrance to the tunnel after a few twists and turns down a dirt road that's really more of a path. Sam jumps out, runs to the side of the forest then returns in a minute. A part of the rock face in front us starts moving upwards at the same pace as a garage door. We drive through, and then the daylight's cut off as the gate rolls back down.

I hit the lights. The sides of the tunnel are smooth, brown earth, and there are wooden supports every few feet. It looks very much like the mining tunnels I've seen in movies, although this one is very wide; probably so they can get Hummers and other vehicles inside.

After maybe ten feet, we hit the top of a hill and the tunnel goes down. It seems to me that Sam floors it, because his Jeep just disappears. I stay at my nice, slow speed even though Cassie frowns at me. It's all fun and games until you take a turn doing ninety and slam into the side of the mountain because you didn't know it was there. Give me the free open highway and then I'll speed.

Twenty minutes later, we hit the bottom of the tunnel and an open steel garage door. I barely drive the Jeep past the opening before the door starts to come down again. Sam waits until it completely closes, and then proceeds at a safer speed. We drive through what is basically the same kind of concrete parking area a mall has then park. Everyone gets out of the vehicles and the doors slam behind us, echoing through the lot.

"How do we get out?" Cassie asks immediately.

Sam gets a curious look on his face.

"We just went through a rough patch. I'm sure you're okay." I raise my hands up in a peace gesture. "But I think we'd both feel better if we know how to get out anytime we'd like."

Sam looks at us for a moment, I think trying to figure out whether to be offended or not, and then nods. "Okay."

We follow him over to a panel on the wall.

"There's one of these panels right next to the overhead door that we came through. To open that door, punch this white button here at the top, then numbers 4, 5 and 6." He mimics the buttons. "To close it, punch the beige button in the middle, followed by 6, 5 and then 4. Got it?"

We both solemnly nod.

"Thank you," I say.

"You're welcome," he replies. Then he leads us to the door to get inside. "There's a camera directly in front of this door and in both corners. From inside, you can pretty much see anyone trying to get in.

"I'll show you how to look at those cameras later on. Always check all angles before letting anyone in, okay? Then, if you're out here, punch in 1-8-9-9." He enters the number and there's a small click. Sam pushes the door open and then smiles over his shoulder. "Come on in."

We walk down a hallway painted in tan tones with tan carpet. I've been walking for maybe a minute when it hits me.

"You have electricity." You would have thought I would have put that together when he was punching neat buttons to let us inside, but what the hey.

"Yeah." He grins at me over his shoulder. "There's an entire field of generators."

"Gas-powered?" I ask, wondering how much gas that would take.

"No. They're solar-powered from panels on the surrounding buildings."

"Wow," I gasp, impressed.

The area we're in looks like an office building. There are light-colored wood doors every few feet. The majority are closed, but the open ones reveal offices, conference rooms, and in some cases the kind of amphitheaters I've seen in movies that are usually shown for college classrooms.

Eventually, the tan carpet and dull hallway end in a circular room that's paved in dark-colored slate tile and has a slate round desk which looks like it should have a receptionist behind it. Sam skirts around the desk and goes to a gray door with another keypad next to it.

"1-7-7-6." He punches the numbers.

"That's corny." Cassie rolls her eyes. He just grins as if so pleased by his own joke that he doesn't care what she thinks.

"Ladies." He holds the door open for us with a flourish. We walk inside with Sunshine's nails clicking on the slate floor, and then he lets the door close behind us with a solid, heavy sound.

This room resembles a family room. There's plush blue carpeting, a leather couch and a couple of gray easy chairs. In front of the sofa are a big-screen TV, an entertainment center, and a PlayStation 3 console, along with a bag of chips and a controller on the floor. The white walls are covered in posters and pictures.

"Some of this was already here, but I brought in the rest."

"Cool," I say. We stand there for a moment, all of us looking at each other, not sure what to do.

"Do you have anything cold to drink?" Cassie asks.

"Sure." Sam heads to the other side of the dining table to a small nook I hadn't noticed when we came in. I follow him over, and it has a small cupboard and one of those really small white refrigerators.

"Water, Coke, or apple juice?"

"Coke!" Cassie exclaims.

He leans into the fridge, one hand on the door, and I can't help but notice that hand seems nice, and strong.

"How about you?" he asks me.

"Oh… Coke, please." I hope he didn't realize I was staring. I take the soda and notice he's grabbed one for himself, as well.

"Thanks." Cassie pops hers open and takes a drink, and now we're all back to staring at each other.

"Hey, would it be okay if I plug in my PSP and play for a bit?"

"Cassie! We just met Sam. Stay for a while and talk." *Dear God, did my mother just speak through me?*

"No, it's cool. Let me show you where you can plug in. I've got a couple of PSP games in there, too," Sam tells her.

I open my Coke and take a long drink, enjoying the cold bite, then walk to the wall filled with pictures. There's a giant poster that says, "Sex Pistols

– Never Mind the Bollocks". Nearby are some photos of a guy decked out in punk outfits who looks like an older version of Sam. In some of the pictures, he's with a group of guys and in another he's with a girl.

I move on and find pictures of Sam. In one, he's little and is standing in front of who can only be his mom and dad. His mom is blonde, thin and has a cute face. His dad is tall and has short brown hair and a serious look about him. Then there's a picture of Sam with a blond boy, both of them standing in front of a forest, and Sam has a huge grin as he holds up bunny ears behind the other boy. Finally, there's a picture of Sam and his dad, neither of them smiling, but holding up a fish together.

"She's all set." Sam comes around the corner.

"Who's he?" I motion toward the blond boy in the picture. Sam walks over, and I'm suddenly very aware of his body next to mine.

"That's James," he says softly.

"He's the one who was supposed to come with you, wasn't he?"

He nods. "My best friend. That was our first trip to the wilderness, ever." He stares at the picture, and I feel bad for asking.

"Your mom's very pretty."

Sam's eyes shift to her. "Thanks."

Well, crap, two for two. So I try something else.

Motioning to the Sex Pistols poster, I ask, "Is that a movie?"

His mouth opens wide, like a gaping fish. Then he closes it and narrows his eyes. "You're messing with me, right?"

"No." I shake my head.

Sam smiles this huge, happy smile. "The Sex Pistols are the best band ever. 'Never Mind the Bollocks' is an album of theirs."

He taps one of the pictures of the guy who looks like Sam. "This is Sid Vicious, the coolest guy in the band."

"He looks a bit like you."

Sam looks at me like I just gave him a shiny ring or some really good chocolate. "You think?"

"Yeah, definitely." I grin.

"Thanks." He smiles, seeming more confident now. He points at the picture with Sid and the girl.

"Sid met this girl named Nancy, and they totally fell in love. Like Romeo and Juliet kind of love, you know?"

I nod.

"They loved each other so much that they couldn't stand being apart. Sid left the band and tried to start a solo career, but they were doing a lot of drugs and that kind of fell apart. So they just did drugs and hung out together. One night he and Nancy got high, and she wound up stabbed and dead. There are some rumors that it might have been someone else, but it looks like he did it."

"Why would he do that?"

Sam shrugs. "In this movie I saw, she kept begging him to kill her. It really looked like an accident more than anything else. It crushed him. He died right after they let him out on bail."

"That's really sad." In the picture, Sid has one arm on Nancy's shoulder, with one eye closed and his fist clenched. He's really skinny. Nancy has blonde, curly hair, and seems to weigh a bit more than Sid, although she isn't fat. She isn't smiling, but has more of a tough, pouty look on her face. I wonder how close to their deaths this picture was taken. It seems amazing and awful all at the same time – a love so strong that it destroyed them both.

"Yeah." Sam nods. "Do you want to hear some of their music?"

"Sure."

Sam bounds over to the stereo, turns it on and hits play. The music is loud, brash and quick. The singer has a unique quality to his voice; not exactly whiny, but definitely unique. It has a good beat, but it's definitely not dance music.

"What do you think?"

"Pretty cool." I smile. *I'll definitely learn to like it*. It has a beat, and I can get into anything with a beat.

"Here's one with Sid singing."

It's a cover of song I recognize: "My Way". The sound quality isn't too good, but I like his voice better than the earlier music. It's more normal, and strong.

Sam goes back to the first album and turns it up. He starts doing that head–thrashing, fake guitar-playing thing guys like to do. I catch the beat, and then I start jumping up and down, occasionally turning in circles and waving my arms.

Hey, look at that. I'm dancing with a guy. Even if it's not at a school dance. Even though the rest of the world is gone.

Here, now, I have a little slice of life.

Chapter 56

After a while, Cassie wanders in and looks at us like we're nuts.

"Can we have lunch now?" she asks.

"Cassie," I admonish, spinning to a halt and breathing hard.

"No, it's okay. I'm getting kind of hungry, too." Sam turns off the music. He heats up hot dogs and mac'n'cheese, then gives paper plates and utensils to Cassie and soda and hot dog buns to me.

"Follow me. I've got something to show you." He grins. We walk back to the reception area and follow the circle to the third door on the right. Sam opens it and reveals a small room that includes an elevator. We go up, eventually coming out in another room with a solid door and a keypad beside it.

"1776," Sam says and Cassie punches in the numbers. The door clicks, and I pull it open and hold it while the others go through.

We're on a roof, decorated with a white plastic patio set in the far right corner with a bright blue sky as a ceiling. Sam heads to the table and Cassie and I follow, putting down the supplies once we reach it. Nearby is a little portable stereo, a bucket full of sand with cigarette butts sticking out and a pair of binoculars lying on the ground next to a rifle. Apparently, Sam likes to come up here a lot.

We dig in. I know hot dogs aren't the finest of foods, but oh, my gosh, this tastes good. That first bite, all warm with ketchup and a soft bun, eaten under a gorgeous blue sky… yum.

I lean back in my chair, sipping from my Coke and eating. The sun warms me right through. This is the life.

I stand up after I'm full. The roof isn't too exciting, but we're on top of one of the main buildings in the complex so I can see a lot of the other buildings from here. It does look more like an academy than a base. Somewhere out there, surely, will be a building full of guns, grenades and more.

And to the northeast I can see a huge mass of zombies, right outside a double row of fences. "Can they get in?"

Sam follows my gaze. "They haven't yet."

I remember the binoculars near the table. "You come up here and watch them, don't you?"

"Yeah," he says. "It's something to do while I'm outside."

"What have you observed?" Cassie asks around a mouthful of hot dog. Sam's eyebrows go up.

"Yeah, she's smart. And a little more mature than other kids," I tell him.

"Yeah," he remarks. "There are two groups: fast and slow. They don't really seem to like to hang out together, but occasionally they will mingle. The slow ones seem to do it by accident, while the fast ones are usually looking for food.

"The slow ones seem completely gone up here." He taps his head. "Nothing really left, just instinct. The fast ones have more of their brains left; more of themselves remain. I've seen different degrees in them, but they're able to move better, grip things, apply some thought to things. They're still not the brightest things on the planet, but there's a spark there. Yeah, a spark."

"Have you seen any that seem to have a spark, but don't move around?" she asks. I realize she's wondering if he's seen any like the town full of zombies we came across.

"Don't move around?" He frowns.

"They just stay still and look at you, sometimes tracking you with their eyes," I add.

His gorgeous brown eyes fill with concern. "No. That sounds creepy. I would definitely notice that. I'll let you know if I see any." He leans back in his chair, still frowning as he bites into another hot dog.

"What about you? What have you guys noticed?"

"About the same." Cassie leans back in her chair. I can't tell if she just doesn't like him, or doesn't trust him. Maybe she's holding back because of last night?

"How about the creepy ones?"

"We came across an entire town like that. They didn't hurt us, just stared at us. Noticed that we were there. All ages: children, adults, all the same."

"Do you think it's possible there are other towns like that?"

Cassie nods slowly.

"Do you think there's anywhere where it's progressed beyond that?"

"What do you mean?" I ask.

"Progressed beyond staring."

"Do you mean progressed, or do you mean they kept more of themselves?" Cassie asks.

"Yes, that's what I mean," Sam clarifies.

"We would probably have to travel the entire country to find out."

"Have you heard anything?" I ask.

"Heard anything?"

"Anything else like this. Have you talked to a lot of people? Have you come across adults?" I question him, and there's a spark of interest in Cassie's eyes. *So last night didn't take away all of her hope then.*

"I've only come across a few people." Sam leans back in his chair, his eyes guarded. "They haven't mentioned anything like the creepy ones."

"And the adults?"

"I only came across a guy in his early twenties. There are rumors, though, of some settlements."

"Really?" Cassie leans forward.

"Just rumors." Sam holds up his hands. "I haven't been able to verify anything yet. There's supposedly one north of Denver, and another near Hoover Dam."

"Hoover Dam?" I ask.

"Electricity," he explains. "There were also brief rumors of people trying to break into NORAD, but I don't know if that succeeded."

"The settlements… can you find out if they really exist?" Cassie grips her chair, her toes digging into the floor.

Chapter 57

Sam is silent for a few moments. Finally, he nods. "There are some things I can try. It'll take a few days, though. In the meantime, would you two like to stay here?"

I hold up a finger to him and lead Cassie to the other side of the roof. The sunshine's just as bright here, and I can see about twenty zombies around the fence that's six blocks away.

"What do you think?" I ask.

"If he can find us a settlement – like the one north of us – that would be great." A huge smile breaks over her face and she's bouncing on her feet. "One with electricity, and a great big lab room, and I could set up my PSP –"

"Yes, but what do you think of *him*? Do you feel safe enough to stay here for a bit?"

She studies Sam, and her face scrunches a bit before she waves her hand. "He's all right. He's weird, but I think he's okay."

I try to see if she's telling the truth, because I'd really like to stay here. I think he's okay, too, but if I'm wrong, and I make this decision and she gets hurt then it's my fault.

"Okay, but if anything happens, just run. You remember the way out and the numbers, right? Just run. You'll come out into the woods and that will be an easy place to hide. Okay?"

Cassie puts her hands on her hips and glares up at me. "I got out just fine on my own last time. You're the one who had trouble."

"You're right. I'm just saying."

"Okay."

We walk back to Sam.

"Thank you. We'd like to stay."

He shades his eyes with his hand and smiles up at me. "Cool."

"I'm playing PSP!" Cassie yells and is running to the door before I can say anything.

I smile and drop into my chair. "Thank you for letting us stay and being so nice to us. It'll be good to be safe for a few days and let her play games."

"That's cool." He shrugs and messes with the arms of his chair. Then he jumps up. "Hey, do you want to look at the zombies?"

"Sure." I shrug, thinking I probably didn't want to.

We stand in the corner of the building and he shows me how to focus the binoculars. I can see two distinct masses: twenty in the group Sam identifies as "slow" and ten in the "fast" group.

"There's one of them out there in the fast group, a guy wearing blue jeans and a short-sleeved white shirt. Blond hair. I catch him watching me a lot."

I move the binoculars through the crowd until I find him in the back, staring up at us. "He moves, right?"

"Yep. I've seen him go after one of the slow ones. And the first time he saw me, he attacked the fence. It's like he saw me and knew I was food." He's smiling and there's a bit of excitement in his voice.

"You're enjoying this, aren't you?"

"What?" He shrugs, but his smile widens.

"This whole predator/prey thing." I gesture to the zombies and then to him.

"We weren't really meant to work in offices and live a safe, regimented life. This is closer to what we're supposed to be."

I sit down on the table and put the binoculars beside me. "Running from place to place without any electricity or food? Scraping by until something kills us?"

"No. Testing our skills against something dangerous. Not scraping by, but really living. Living with danger and adrenaline, like we're supposed to.

Not shut away in little boxes."

"Those boxes protect us." *How on Earth do I keep getting surrounded by people who jump into risks?*

"Those boxes keep us from living. Come on, how alive were you before all of this?"

I think of my mom. I think of us laughing on the couch together, happy for a few minutes.

"I was alive." I shove off the table and walk away from him. I'm about halfway across the roof before he catches up, grabbing my wrist to get me to stop.

"Hey, I'm sorry. I didn't mean to bug you. I'm just saying that the adrenaline rush that comes with an attack…that didn't happen a lot before. Know what I mean?"

I think of those times when I wasn't afraid, when I won and stood alive over something that had just tried to eat me. Yeah, I know what he's talking about.

"Yeah," I admit grudgingly.

"It's okay to like it. It's kept us alive. It means you're strong."

No one's ever called me strong before. "Yeah?" I ask.

"Yeah." He smiles. "Now, you wanna go play some video games?"

"Sure."

As we head back down, I realize that he's thinks I'm strong, which means I'll have to hide from him that I'm really a coward. Crap.

Chapter 58

I jolt awake in a dark, unfamiliar room. I'm sure it's still the middle of the night, but I don't know what woke me up. I stay still, trying to figure it out. I don't hear anything huge and crashing, so I don't think we're being attacked.

Then I hear it. Moans. Long, crying zombie moans. More than one voice, more than one sound.

My fingers dig into the blankets. Oh, God, I thought we were actually safe. I thought I'd found a place where I could truly sleep for a few nights at least.

Moving slowly so I can stay quiet, I lean over and drag the bat out from under the bed. I get up and go to the door. My hand pauses over the knob, heart pounding. Not even one night inside and I'm already back to being this nervous?

I steel myself, remind myself to be strong, and fling the door open, bat at the ready. I don't see anything there. I sidle out into the hallway, looking both ways, but find nothing.

God, but I hear those moans. So mournful.

Maybe they're on the other side of that huge safety door?

I head toward the living room with a bit of a quicker pace, going down a dark hallway full of closed doors until I get to one with a flickering light.

The moans are right here. I raise my bat and step into the room.

There's a bank of monitors in front of me, along with a desk, a chair, and a puzzled Sam.

"Are you going to hit me?"

I lower the bat. "No. I was going to hit the zombies I was hearing."

"Oh, they're just on the screen." He motions to the wall of monitors behind him. I walk closer, dragging the bat behind me.

There are ten displays, all with different views of the complex, all of them filled with zombies. On one of the screens is a young woman. Her eyes are clear of cracks, but the whites are replaced by blue. I can see dark blue veins above her shirt. She's staring straight ahead, and for a moment I feel that she can see me. A shudder ripples through me and I turn away.

"You can hear them? Why did you turn the sound on?"

"Why not?" Sam shrugs.

"Doesn't it freak you out?"

"Eh." He shrugs. "They can't get me. And you never know what you might hear."

"Are you thinking they might talk, or that you might hear someone scream?"

"After what you and Cassie mentioned about the creepy ones, I wouldn't be surprised if a zombie popped up that could talk. If it's someone screaming, I won't get there in time to help them, but I might get there in time to help their friends."

He pulls a chair with wheels out from under the desk. "Go ahead and sit down."

I sit on the edge of the chair, still gripping my bat. I notice there's a Coke can and a bag of chips on the desk and gingerly reach in and take one.

Crunching, I look from screen to screen. There seem to be a lot of families. There's one young mother, maybe in her twenties, wearing a torn brown sweater and a blue jean skirt. She's covered in blood and holding her kindergartner's hand. There's a bite mark on her cheek, a couple more on her forearms, and bits of cracked skin beneath that. She looks like she fought like hell, and I bet she did it all to protect her kid. The little girl holding her hand has on a matching outfit and curly brown hair. I don't see any bite marks or blood on the child; just cracked blue eyes and cracked skin.

"Are a lot of the little kids attacked, or do they just seem to be infected?" I point at the pair.

"I think the majority of the tiny ones I've seen are just infected. I'm not sure how that works." He shrugs. I've been seeing the same thing, and I don't have a reason why either.

"Me too," I agree.

Going from screen to screen, I think to myself that this is humanity now. Our violence is out for the entire world to see, but even our ability to love is visible in one undead hand curled around another.

What about our ability to innovate? How will that appear in the new species we've born?

"Do they sleep? Do they recover?" I ask. What I'm really thinking is do they do anything other than search for food? Will this be a desperate race to the end for survivors, or is this truly a new species?

"I haven't seen any of them sleep yet. As to recovery, I don't know yet."

I realize he hasn't been looking at the screen for a while. He drags my chair over to him by the arm and I laugh a bit, not sure what he's doing.

He picks up my hand, running his fingers along my palm. Then before I realize what he's doing, he leans in and kisses me.

It's soft and gentle and not at all what I thought my first kiss might be like. He stops and pulls back, and asks quietly, "Okay?"

I nod, not really sure what to say. He kisses me again, and this time I'm prepared enough to worry about it. Am I doing this right? Is it okay? He doesn't say anything, so I think so.

Eventually my nervousness fades, and his hands touch my face, and then we stop. I look at him, and his face is so close to mine, and his eyes are shining. I don't want him to stop.

"You're trembling," he states, and I realize it's true. I don't know why, so I just nod. He leans in and kisses my forehead, then gives me a hug.

"Come on. Let's get you back to bed." He leads me back to my room.

"Did I do something wrong?" I ask quietly. He looks at me, startled, then smiles.

"No," he says, and we kiss again. It's nice and soft and slow, and I can't imagine anything better.

"Now go to sleep, and tomorrow I'll show you how to kill zombies with something other than a bat."

Chapter 59

In the morning we're back on the roof with Sam, setting up paper targets held in little metal boxes. I walk back a bit and he hands me something that looks a bit like my shotgun but doesn't quite feel the same.

"What's this?" I ask.

"It's a BB gun."

"I've been using a real gun."

"And been missing, right?"

"Yeah, but –"

"Yeah, but I don't want you missing and shooting your foot or me. A BB's a lot easier to deal with than a bullet."

"Yeah, okay." I roll my eyes.

"Go ahead and show me how you've been shooting."

I put the end of the gun against my shoulder, try to aim and then pull the trigger. There is some kick but it doesn't exactly hurt; it's startling more than anything. There's a bit of noise, too.

We both walk to the target and kneel down to look at it. I pick it up and examine it, but I can't find any sign of the BB.

"Where is it?"

"Out there somewhere." He points off the end of the building. "You missed it completely."

I make a face at him.

"Come on back and I'll show you a few things."

I walk back and act like I'm going to shoot again. Gently, he turns my waist a bit and then repositions my fingers.

"When it comes time to fire, gently squeeze the trigger. Another way to think of it is to roll the trigger back." He stands behind me, looking over my shoulder as I fire again. We walk back to the target.

"Hey! I shot it!" I point proudly to the mark on the edge of the paper.

"Good job." He smiles. "Now let's try to improve that aim."

We walk back and I shoot again. I do about the same, just in different spots, a couple of more times.

"So what do you think is throwing you off?" he asks.

Thinking about it, I raise the gun and aim. "It seems like every time I try to focus on the spot I want the gun wobbles a bit."

"Very good. We think we hold things still, but

really we don't. We kind of shift all the time and just don't see it. So try a very tight grip on the gun, and then before you're about to shoot, hold your breath."

I tighten my grip, line up my sight, and take a huge, deep breath. Then I slowly squeeze the trigger. I hurry to the target, my heart jumping from the excitement. This time, my BB hit the circle around the inner ring – much closer to the bulls-eye than ever before.

"Much better!" Sam says, and I grin.

He sets up another target, and then we both shoot for a while. By the time we finish, I'm hitting the bulls-eye every once in a while.

"Thank you, Sam! That's much better!"

"You're a good student." He smiles. "Now before we go in, let's try one more time, with a real gun, pointing at a real target."

"Do you mean one of the zombies?"

He nods.

"Wow, okay."

He leads me back over to the far corner with the picnic table. On the ground are more guns, and this time they look more like what I've seen in movies. Some of them even have scopes. Sam hands me one.

"What is this called?"

"Do you really want to know, and will you really remember it?"

I think about it and then grin. "No, not really. Kind of like with cars."

"Uh-huh, that's what I thought. It's the pretty black gun, then," he says.

"Dork." I give him a dirty look, but he just grins.

"Look through the scope first."

I comply, and point at the zombies. Oh, God. I can see them pretty well. I scan the crowd, flowing through the slow ones until I come to a male that's standing still. His fingers grip the fence, and except for the big hunk of flesh hanging from his cheek he reminds me a lot of my third grade teacher. I didn't like my third grade teacher much.

"Find one?"

"Yeah," I tell him while trying not to move much.

"Then squeeze the trigger. The kick will be a bit more."

I slowly squeeze and he's right; there's definitely more of an impact on my shoulder. "Did I get him?"

"Look through the scope."

"I think I got him in the shoulder." I point. Sam borrows the scope from me and follows where I'm pointing.

"Not bad. Not bad at all. I think you're going to be good at this."

"Thanks." I like that look in his eyes, the one that says I did something right.

Then it hits me. There's something missing. Some *one* missing.

"Hey, where's Cassie?"

Chapter 60

I lead the way down to the main living area.

"Cassie!" I call. The family room is deserted so I keep going. I walk back to the little PSP room but it's dark too. Sam's a couple of feet behind me as I head to her room. The light's still on, the twin bed's unmade and her backpack is open and on top of her pillow.

"Well, her stuff is still here, so she hasn't like left-left, but she's gone," I say.

"Anything missing?" Sam asks, standing in the doorway.

A lot of her stuff is still packed, but I can see her PSP charging on the brown chest of drawers to my left. I root around in the backpack.

"I don't notice anything missing." I sit back and think. Where would she have gone? I absentmindedly start playing with my necklaces and my fingers touch the USB drive.

"You said this used to be an academy, right?"

"Yeah."

"Would they have science stuff? Like science classrooms, labs, biology labs?"

"Yeah. They actually did some research here, too."

"That's it!" I grin. "She's headed to the labs."

"Why? What would a kid want with a lab?"

I realize this might not be something I should tell him. Weird, I let him kiss me, but I'm not sure I can trust him with the truth about Cassie's dad. What if he gets all angry and tries to hurt her? I lean back on my hands and look up at him. Better to tell him now instead of when we're trying to find her and he has a gun.

"Cassie's dad developed The Shot."

"The Shot? The one that was supposed to save everybody?"

"Yeah." I study his face, looking for signs of anger. I don't know him very well, but I don't see any.

"Wow." He sits down heavily next to me on the bed.

"Yeah. A... crowd came to the house afterwards. He had a caretaker sneak Cassie out the back while he went out front. He died saving her."

"God, that sucks."

"Yeah. Please be careful when talking about it

with her, okay? It hit her pretty hard. I think they were really close. And don't tell anyone else."

"I won't," he says, still in thought. "So, when you say they were close, was she there when he was developing The Shot?"

"Yeah, for part of it." I'm not sure how much to tell him, so I decide to leave most of it up to Cassie. "She thinks he was close."

"To a cure?"

"No." I shake my head. "First, to prevent people from catching it. Then the next step would be a cure."

"Wouldn't the infected just die from their wounds?"

"We don't know. Probably. But it might help some of the kids who don't have any wounds."

"Good point." He nods. "So, we should probably find her and help her out, huh?"

"Definitely." I reply, relieved he isn't angry about Cassie's connection to The Shot. "I'm worried about her being out there alone. Let's bring guns, okay?"

"Hey, look who likes having a gun now." He smiles. "Yeah, that's cool, but you have to go in front so you don't shoot me accidentally."

I roll my eyes. "Yeah, okay, whatever. You just don't want to be the first in the door."

"Well, why should I? I've got a sharpshooter with me now."

"Uh-huh," I say. "Come on." I grab his hand and pull him to his feet. Funny how it always takes me so long to get used to touching people, except for Sam.

He leads me to a room full of weapons, giving me a handgun to slip into the waist of my jeans and a shotgun, as well.

"Don't shoot your foot," he orders. I give him a dirty look and then we head out.

Chapter 61

We walk on the emptied pathways of the former academy. Everything is silent, ghostly, like at any moment a bell might ring and a bunch of students will come streaming out, chatting and laughing.

"Where do you think the lab's at?"

Sam shrugs in response. We walk quietly for a few minutes until we reach a crossroads. We randomly pick a direction and wander up and down the paths like that for twenty minutes until we find a four-story tan brick building with a set of double doors open at the front.

"Want to try in there?" I ask and Sam nods.

Inside, it's cool and dark with all of the doors closed and the blinds drawn. Sam digs into his pocket, pulls out a small flashlight and clicks it on.

It looks like any school, with classroom after classroom. I even peek into some of them, but Cassie isn't there.

"Cassie?" I call out tentatively, but don't hear anything back. About a block into the school, we hit a set of very wide, stately stairs, with a branch leading up and another leading down. Taking a wild guess, I head down the stairs, Sam at my side.

"So, who taught you to shoot?" I ask.

"My Dad, back when he cared," Sam answers, staring straight ahead. I don't even know what to say to that. *Sorry your dad became a dick?*

"What happened?"

"After he and my mom divorced, he didn't really want a lot to do with us. Same old story."

"New family?"

He shakes his head. "New career. Not a lot of time for us anymore." He shrugs, like it doesn't matter.

"My parents divorced, too. My Dad moved out to California. Divorce sucks." It's all I can think of to say. Sam nods.

We turn a corner, and at the end of the hall is a Jeep parked sideways against an open door. I walk closer and I can see blood on the windshield and on the side of the door.

"What the hell?" Sam asks. He vaults into the Jeep. "Keys are still in it."

I don't see anything in the room beyond, and there doesn't seem to be a lot of explanation as to why the vehicle is here. Was it to keep something out, or something in? If so, it wouldn't make sense that the door's wide open.

Why did they leave it this way? What happened?

I have the feeling that I will go through life seeing signs of others without ever finding out what happened to them.

Sam can't open the door on the other side, and we can't jump over the thing, so we decide to crawl under it. The floor is wet, not from blood but from something else, and it does look like someone else scuttled through. I'm hoping it was Cassie; I would hate to go through this muck twice for no reason.

It's a bit darker under the Jeep, but I can see a bit into the next room. The laminated floors look like they could be a part of a cafeteria, but that just could be my perspective.

Something grabs my foot, and I let out a short sound that isn't quite a scream. I twist and find Sam laughing.

"You jerk!" I kick at him and he just laughs harder.

"That was a great scream," he says.

I finish crawling out from under the Jeep and he follows.

"Yeah, and I'm sure everything in the surrounding area heard me, too." I cross my arms and cock a hip.

"Nothing's in here." He shrugs.

And that's when I hear the sound of pounding feet.

Chapter 62

"Fast ones," I say, just as zombies pour into the room from two doors in front of us – one on the east and one on the west side.

"Run!" Sam shouts, pointing at a door north of us.

The zombies hit the middle of the room the same time as me. On my right side is a young woman in a long brown skirt and a tan top. Her throat's ripped out, but she doesn't seem to notice. On my left is a huge man – made of muscle instead of fat – who has hair so short I can't tell the color. He's wearing dirty jeans and a formerly white t-shirt, and is bitten all over, like it took a pack of zombies to take him out.

He grabs my arm so hard it yanks me fully around, his grip so strong it hurts. Brown, shining eyes burn into me and his mouth opens wide. Without really thinking about it, I raise my hand and find I'm holding a gun. The whole thing feels like a reflex, like jumping on a bike. I put it right to his open mouth and pull the trigger.

The sound seems loud in this enclosed room, and I don't see the zombies that must be near me. I just see the light in his eyes go away and feel things splatter me.

Something else grabs my arm and I scream, whirling around with the gun in my hand. Sam's eyes are wide but he holds up one hand.

"Come on!" he shouts, and then releases me so he can shoot the woman closing in. Together, we race to the other side and through the big open doorway.

"Shit, shit, shit!" Sam yells, as we both realize there isn't a door to close. We run down the hallway, zombies streaming after us, Sam's shoes squeaking on the floor. I gesture with my gun to a door at the end of the hallway. He nods.

"Go faster."

I speed up with my last reserves as he slows down a bit. I put the gun in my other hand and yank on the doorknob, praying it isn't locked. It turns and I run through, holding it open for Sam.

"Come on!"

He shoots one near him, kicks another, and then races past me. I slam the door shut and throw the bolt home just as a body thuds into it.

"Good job." Sam grins. "In normal times, never run with a gun when the safety's off."

I roll my eyes and try to hide the fact that my

heart is trying to jump out of my chest.

"Sure."

"Come on," he says, and we lope off down the hallway.

"She can't have come down here," I tell him.

"Why not?"

I motion backwards. "Zombie hell?"

"She was probably quiet."

"Hey, I wasn't the one who grabbed someone's leg."

"No, you're just the one who screamed." He grins. I push him so he stumbles, and he laughs again.

"Hey, I think we're in the right place." I motion to the room to my right. The open door shows what looks like a chemistry lab from school – black desks, beakers and all.

We keep going and the labs start to get nicer and more sophisticated. Then I hear the soft humming of a Lady Gaga song.

"Cassie," I call out, and run in the direction of the song.

Chapter 63

I find her in a white lab which looks similar to the one I saw in her house. There's a long, steel table that resembles an autopsy table and near that is a narrow hospital bed with straps attached. There's a sink about five feet behind the bed, and then a row of tables to the right.

Cassie's back is to us and she's rifling through a set of drawers.

"Cassie," I say and her shoulders hunch. She stops and turns around. "What are you doing here? Why didn't you tell me you were coming here?"

"You were busy," she answers, but she stares at the floor.

"Why did you come here?"

Her eyes flick to Sam and then back to the ground. "I was looking for something."

"What?"

She looks at him again but still doesn't answer.

"I told him about your dad and The Shot," I admit. She glares at me and crosses her arms.

"What?" I raise my hands and then let them drop. "You ran off without telling us anything. The only place I could think to look for you was the labs, and how was I supposed to explain that?"

She kicks the legs of the table in front of her. "You should have asked."

"You should have told me where you were going."

She glares at me again. "You're not my mother."

"No, I'm your friend." I cross my arms. How could she not realize that I would worry?

"Okay, guys." Sam steps between us with his hands up. "There's a whole bunch of zombies behind us, so let's just get what you came for and get out."

The anger building on Cassie's face slips away. "Zombies? There are zombies free?"

"Yeah. What do you mean by free?" I ask.

She gestures to the left with her head. "Go check out the zombie zoo."

There's something in the way she says it that tells me she's still a bit mad at me. I'm mad at her, too, so that works. Let Sam help her with what she needs. I leave the room and go to the left.

I walk down a long, white hall with white tiles. Halfway down, there's a window into a room on my left. Something slams into the glass and I jump a bit.

It's a zombie, its bloody hands streaking blood all over the pane. Its blue eyes are cracked but there's a film over them, giving the eyes a cloudy look. The flesh has a bit of that cracked look as well, but overall the empty-head seems doughy, like the flesh was soft and flat before, and then becoming a zombie made the whole body swell. Its eyes don't even seem to follow me; it's more like it sort of sensed my presence and slammed itself against the window. The rest of the room behind it is dark, but I see shapes moving behind it. My best guess is that there are others in there but they're not bright enough to even sense that I'm here.

I watch its open, gaping mouth, letting my heart calm down and my breathing even out, and then I move on, walking much slower this time.

The next room is lit, and is filled with zombies in the slow range of what I'm used to. They notice me and shuffle to the window, slamming themselves against the glass, their eyes staring at me the whole time. There are three men and two women. The men are all dressed alike in khakis and white, button-down shirts while the women are wearing white lab coats, slacks and pretty blouses. One of the women has glasses on a chain hanging down her shirt. Her eyes are brown, so it's harder to see the virus in them, but her brown skin is cracked like Texas mud in the summer. There's a whole chunk missing out of her neck and blood down her front.

Her hand slams the window.

The glass holds, and I decide to walk further down the hall.

I see now why Cassie called this a zombie zoo. I pass room after room filled with different types. I reach a room holding a bunch of fast ones; they rush the window and hit it so hard it shudders. I watch it and the wall for a bit, wondering if they will give, but everything holds. They pound on the window and then I see one of them glance at a door to his left. He's wearing a brown sweater, nice dark-brown pants and a white lab coat. He's younger, probably in his thirties when he died, and his eyes still snap with some intelligence. Yes, there's definitely still a spark in there.

He runs to the door and actually turns the knob. I grip the gun stuck in the front of my jeans, ready to shoot if necessary. The door doesn't move, and he slams his fist against it. I jump a bit. He runs back to the window, as if to see if I'm still there. I walk away, but I can still feel his eyes on me as I go down the hall.

I pass a lot more rooms like that, until I come to the end of the hallway and there's just one more room left.

It's lit inside, revealing cabinets and a black countertop against the far wall and a black table in the middle of the room. There's a female sitting on the table, facing away from me. She's in one of those white hospital gowns with an open back, and I can see her pale white skin leading down to her white underwear.

I take a step closer and she turns, almost like she knew I was there. *Did she hear me? Could she hear me through the glass?*

She turns in a really neat maneuver, so her legs are still closed and she doesn't flash me. She pulls the gown tight and looks up at me.

The front of the gown is decorated with little red apples. She has black hair, with flashes of blue glinting in it as she moves. Her black eyes reveal only a tiny bit of the virus. I step closer and that's when I see her skin isn't cracked. Instead there are silver lines, cool threads showing through her skin. It's almost like her veins or arteries are showing – with that same random trace of lines – but the colors are silver instead of red or blue.

I realize then that she hasn't rushed the windows like the others. She isn't desperately trying to get to me.

Her black eyes burn with intelligence. She notices my open-mouthed stare, and this closed-mouth smile spreads slowly across her face. Her hands grip the edge of the table and she starts swinging her legs.

She is a zombie, and yet she is completely, totally aware. Her intelligence is intact.

Chapter 64

My heart's pounding as I slowly raise my palm to the glass, just to see if she will respond.

"Delilah!" Sam shouts and I jump. "Come on! We're ready to go!" He stands at the far end of the hallway and waves me toward him.

I take one last quick glance at the girl as her smile deepens and her legs swing. I have an odd thought then. She isn't concerned about reaching me at all. Does that mean she isn't hungry? Does that mean she could last forever in there?

"Delilah!"

Reluctantly, I turn away and jog to Sam. "Did you find what she needed?"

"We found one thing and I think I can find the rest back home."

"Really?"

"Yeah, just a little bit of hacking." He shrugs.

"Cool."

We reach the lab and find Cassie waiting for us. "Sorry," she apologizes, glancing quickly at me and then back down at the floor.

"Me, too," I say, and surprise myself by giving her a quick hug. She squeezes back as I pull away.

"That's great, guys, but now we've got to get past the zombies."

"There weren't any the way I came in."

"Which way?"

She points in the opposition direction of how we came in.

"Great. Lead the way," I tell her.

She steers us down another white hallway, this time without any labs or empty-heads, but just classroom after classroom. She takes a left and heads up a small concrete stairway. At the top, she hits the panic bar on a brown door to the right and then we're outside.

"Ah." I breathe in fresh air. "That was much easier." We head back to the living area.

"How did you guys come in?"

"There are a couple of doors open on the other side. We came in through those, went down some stairs, went past a Jeep and then found a bunch of zombies in a cafeteria."

"Wow." Her eyes widen. "Hey, Sam, I thought the compound was empty of them?"

Sam shrugs. "We checked out the area where I've

been living, but I didn't explore the other buildings yet. Kind of glad I didn't now."

"We?" I ask.

"There were three of us. My friend James, me, and Steve. Steve was in the military. He knew about this place."

"How did you know him?"

"We met him through an outreach program – you know, one of those things where they try to get bad kids to go straight and do good things when they grow up."

"You were a bad kid?"

"Poor, troubled, whatever." He shrugs again and looks away.

Cassie, who's been skipping ahead, races back and grabs a hand from each of us. "Come on. I want to find this stuff out."

Sam grins, and we let her pull us back home.

Once we're back inside, Sam leads us to a room past our bedrooms. It looks like it was originally a bedroom, but now it's filled with computers. He plops down in a chair at a desk, hits the keyboard and two screens come to life in front of him.

"So, what did you find?" I ask Cassie. She reaches into her back pocket and pulls out a rumpled piece of paper.

I smooth it out and read. It's like an acceptance letter or something – full of sentences like "we're so happy to work with you" and "we think we'll accomplish great things on this project". It's signed Consortium Pharmaceuticals but the letterhead at the top reads Pharmaceux.

"What's Pharmaceux?" I hand the paper back to Cassie.

"It's a drug company."

We sit down on the floor while Sam pounds frantically on the keyboard, occasionally swearing.

"Drugs, huh?" I think it over. "Does this have something to do with The Shot?"

"Exactly." Cassie smiles. "Sam's looking for more evidence."

"Evidence of what?" I glance at Sam.

"It's okay." She waves her hand and takes a deep breath. "I don't think my Dad fully created The Shot."

Chapter 65

"What do you mean by *fully*?" I narrow my eyes.

"I don't think he started from scratch. I think he was given something to start with."

"Why do you say that?"

"They just gave him vials of blood. It all started before India. They said they wanted him to look for a cure for a virus. That's what he told me. But what if some of those vials were what they had developed as a cure? What if they could only get so far and needed him to step in?"

"What would it matter if he created all of The Shot or only some of it?"

"My dad was one of the best in the world at this, Delilah. Yeah, he didn't have a lot of time to work on it, but The Shot was a complete failure. That's not like him."

"You want to clear his name."

"Yes."

I don't point out that there are so few people left that it doesn't matter. It matters to her, so it's important. Then something snaps in place in my head. "You led us here, didn't you? You never wanted to go to Garden of the Gods."

She looks down at the carpet. "I'm sorry. Please don't be mad."

"Why didn't you just tell me?"

She picks at the rug. "What if he really was a failure?"

Before I met Cassie, I'd blamed her dad for The Shot's false promise. But after knowing her, I gave him the benefit of the doubt. I mean, how likely was it that anyone could create something that would protect us from the virus that quickly? But thinking about it now, and seeing the hurt on her face, I realize I wouldn't want to talk about it, either. If he was my dad, I wouldn't want to do a side trip that risked our lives only to find out he did really fail.

"He raised a good daughter. He protected you and saved your life. Whatever else he was or did, he was a good guy."

She hugs me, squeezing my arms against my sides. I gently pat her with my fingers. "So, what's Sam doing?"

"He's trying to find out if he can locate anything in the system about the project and my dad's involvement."

"Cool."

We're there for a while, eventually pulling out a deck of cards and playing gin rummy until Sam slaps his hand on the desk, startling me.

"Pay-dirt," he says.

"What?" Cassie jumps up and leans over him, peering at the monitor, and Sam frowns and pushes her back away from him.

"We'll all have laptops in a bit – we're going to need it. The main set of servers had a butt-load of security on them. It took me a while, but I eventually found a development server – a computer used for testing – which looks like it has a ton of email archives and documents from a whole group of people in this research area. I can set up a few computers with this information and then we can start digging through, if somebody will make some dinner?" He grins.

"I will." Cassie jumps up and down.

"*We* will," I correct, because I want to have more than cereal.

"Great." Sam turns away and starts madly typing.

Sam has set up two more desks with computers by the time we return with plates of macaroni and cheese, chicken nuggets and beans. He takes a few minutes to show us how to look at everything, and then we start digging.

Well after dinner, Cassie says, "Hey, I found something."

We both rush over to look over her shoulder. It's a welcoming letter to her dad, similar to the printed letter we found.

"That's a few months before India," Sam points out.

"Who wrote it?" I ask.

"Michael Cavendish," Cassie responds.

"Start looking for him, as well," I reply. Sam and I sit back down again and we all get back to work.

I keep thinking about it, though. If these people came to Cassie's dad to help with The Shot, why did they have it in the first place? Did they find the first zombie? How and why did India happen?

Chapter 66

I don't know what's up with my section, but it's all boring stuff, with a lot of notes and agendas from meetings. Before I can totally fall asleep Sam puts on a random mix of songs, and that and a Coke wake me up a bit.

Hours later my eyes hurt, and I rub them a bit and look up. Sam catches my eye, puts a finger in front of his lips and motions to Cassie, who's fallen asleep with her head on the desk. He points to him, then me, and then to the door.

I nod and close another document, my eye catching a phrase at the last moment: the Amelia project. I make a mental note to look further into that when I get back, and quietly get up and meet Sam outside the room.

We go up to the roof and I sit down on the edge, swinging my legs off the side and sipping from my Coke. Sam sits next to me.

"That is boring –"

"As shit." He cuts me off and we grin at each other.

"Yeah, but it's important to her."

"Man, I never realized how boring corporate life was until now."

"Tell me about it. I've been reading through meeting notes."

"Find anything interesting?"

"Not really. Just one thing I need to look into: the Amelia Project. How about you?"

He shrugs. "All mine is military stuff. I think I might be getting close, though."

"Military? What does that have to do with a drug company?"

"Army needs drugs, too." He grins.

"Yeah." We fall silent, listening to the random zombie moans and a few crickets. It's warm and peaceful. If I totally block out the empty-heads, we could just be up on the roof of the mall, hanging out after a long day of shopping. Well, except for the fact that Sam is a guy, and I'm not sure how often guys spend all day shopping.

"You did really well today," Sam says. "You were really brave, looking for Cassie and getting her out of there." His fingers lightly trace up and down my arm and I shiver.

"You were there, too."

"Yeah, I was," he agrees and leans in for a kiss.

I kiss him back and everything else slips away. I forget there are zombies wanting to kill me, I forget about looking through the computers, I forget about everything but the warm night and Sam.

We stop to breathe and he's just smiling at me, and I feel beautiful and special with him looking at me like that.

"And now the reward for our bravery." He reaches into his back pocket, taking out a little piece of paper and filling it with little bits of green.

"I've never seen anyone roll their own cigarette before," I say.

"Yeah." He grins, seals it and lights it. He takes a deep drag, closing his eyes for a moment, and then slowly lets the smoke out.

"Oh, yeah," he says again and hands it to me.

I get it up to my mouth and stop. I can feel the heat between my fingers, and I've smelled this scent before.

Time slows down and I remember this smell. I remember this smell coming out of Mike's room a lot, months before he changed. I remember the giggles when I would walk into his room, from him and his friends. I remember that after I learned this smell my brother stopped hanging out with me.

With this smell, everything changed.

I hold this burning thing in my hand and wonder what I'm going to do, even as the first tear slides down my face.

Chapter 67

I shake a bit inside. Sam's been so nice to me, and we get along really well. I want to please him, I do. But oh, God, I can't do this again. I've been through this before; I lost someone through this before.

Might as well lose him early.

I lean forward and open my fingers, letting the cigarette that's not a cigarette fall, over the edge and into the darkness. Tears flood down my face, and Sam is already shouting as I reach around him, grab the bag of weed and then that sails into the darkness, too. Then everything catches up to me again.

"What the fuck are you doing?" Sam shouts. He's standing up, leaning over as if he can follow the marijuana over the side safely. I hunch into myself, like I used to do when my dad yelled, but then I remember that Sam's not my dad. I roll away and come to a stand, hugging myself.

"That was weed."

"Exactly," Sam says. "Why the fuck did you throw it off the roof?"

"Weed's bad." I swipe at my tears and feel sick inside my chest.

"Weed's bad? Really? What are you, five?"

This fire rushes through me, burning away the sick, weak feeling in my chest. "Five? You think I'm five? We're surrounded by zombies and you're doing something that alters your perception of reality? Really?" My arms drop to my sides.

"We're fine. They're all the way over there, behind a fence." He thrusts a finger behind him.

"Yeah, and you thought the compound was empty of zombies until this morning!"

"You're fucking nuts. We're fine up here, Delilah!"

"No, we're not. We're not fine and we're not safe. We just have that illusion. We need to keep our wits."

"I need to relax. I don't know about you, Delilah, but I can't keep going like this all the time!"

"You can't? Or are you just used to being high?" This is getting ugly. I don't like the way he's looking at me right now. His face is twisted and angry.

"Get out of my sight." He turns his back to me.

"Fine." I stalk toward the door and then stop. "Believe it or not, Sam, you're better than this. You're better than this and you're smarter than this.

You made it through a world of zombies and you're alive. Stop being stupid, and stop trying to kill yourself because you made it through."

"I'm not –"

He's shouting as I slam the door behind me. I'm shaking and crying as I run down the steps. I make it down to my bedroom and slam the door, throwing myself onto the bed as the tears get so thick the room is blurry.

And then I realize a part of what I just said to Sam is what I really wanted to say to my brother.

Chapter 68

Mike was a normal, fun kid with great grades all through elementary school. He wasn't popular and he wasn't an outcast; he had a nice group of friends who let me hang out with them, too.

The summer before middle school Mike's best friend, Brian, moved to Chicago. I remember Mike being nervous the week before middle school, and wondering if he would find a new best friend.

He made it through the first week just fine, without being thrown in a locker or getting in a fight, and then the Friday of the second week he brought someone new home.

The new guy was named Dean. He had medium-length blond hair, the remnants of a tan, and clear, cold blue eyes. He would smile at you without the smile lighting his eyes, and in fact they always looked a bit off, a bit dead, whether he was smiling or not. Looking into his eyes always gave me a bit of the heebie-jeebies, so after a while I avoided it.

Dean was very pleasant when he first met us. He was on the soccer team, a bit athletic, and was always wearing flip-flops which showed off the hairy tops of his feet. My mom was really impressed with him at first, but then she was working outside of the house and didn't see what was going on.

Dean got my brother high from the very first time he came over. That first afternoon I flew into my brother's room right after school, anxious to share my day with him, and Dean washed all over my excitement like a cold bucket of water. He lay in my brother's bed, smoking weed and grinning at me with his lazy, cold smile as we were introduced.

Then he got my brother high again and again.

Soon Dean, my brother, and a mix of kids were getting high every afternoon. Gradually, my brother's old friends stopped coming by. The new friends were loud, dirty, and not really nice. I stopped going in there.

After a while, my parents stopped liking Dean. They found out a bit more about him and what was going on. Then, Dean stopped coming around, and I found out from other kids why – Dean went to juvie for dealing drugs.

With relief, I waited for my brother to come back, but instead the afternoon parties continued.

Then one day, I came home and found the house

mostly silent. My parents weren't home, and the flow of kids from the kitchen to Mike's room was absent. So I went to his door and knocked. I waited a few minutes but didn't get an answer, so I decided to go in anyways.

Mike was sitting on the floor cross-legged, all by himself. The room wasn't full of smoke. But for some reason, my heart started pounding.

"Hi, Mike," I greeted.

He looked up at me and there was a goofy smile on his face. His eyes weren't focused, really; instead, he looked like he was trying really hard not to fall asleep. I snapped my fingers within inches of his face and he didn't even flinch.

"Mike, what are you on?" This hard, angry voice came out of me, and I didn't even recognize myself.

His grin widened into a smile and he tried to make letters out of his fingers, but they didn't work properly.

"Ahhhh," he finally said, gave a bit of a guffaw, and then he forgot I was there.

I stood still, and saw my brother forget I was there. I looked into his stupid, goofy, unfocused eyes and saw it happen.

My brother became a zombie long before it was popular.

Chapter 69

There's a knock on the door. I open it and find Sam outside.

"Please, let me in."

I leave it open and then flounce onto the bed. Sam shuts the door, sits on the bed and hugs me.

I really wasn't expecting that.

"I'm sorry I yelled," he apologizes. He's quiet for a few moments, resting his head against mine. "You care about me."

I'm not sure if that's a question or not. I pull back so I can see his eyes.

"Yes, I care about you." How can he not know that? I hug him, the look in his eyes bugging me. It's like he thought I might say no, that I might kick him. Then there's this other part, this warm part that starts blossoming in his eyes as soon as I say yes.

His arms tighten around me and he pulls us both

backward until we're stretched out on the bed, cuddling.

We're quiet for a long while, and then gradually I tell him about my brother. I tell him parts I never told anyone else, not even my parents.

He hugs me as I cry. I may not ever be able to fix things with Mike, but getting it out, telling my friend and hearing him say it's okay, makes me feel better.

Eventually I stop crying, and I'm beginning to think he might have fallen asleep when I feel him kiss my hair, and he starts to talk quietly.

"When my parents divorced, it was like my family just melted beneath me. My parents went off in different directions and I was the only one left. I lived with my mom for a while, but she was either at work or with her new boyfriend. They packed up and moved to Montana, and she sent me to my dad's house so I could stay at the same school.

"Dad got married six months after the divorce to this blonde chick who wasn't anything like Mom. She didn't really know how to act around me. My dad went to work and left me with her. Said he had to spend extra time at work to help his career.

"I would get in trouble at school and he didn't care. Blondey showed up because they called her. She'd bitch because she missed work.

"I got into some trouble and wound up in juvie for a few days. After they let me out, they sent me to foster care for a while, and we had family counseling. That's where I met James.

"First person in a while who cared. Like you." He hugs me against him. "James was cool. Knew things, knew how to be. He had a family like mine and it didn't even faze him. He showed me a bunch of stuff. Then we met Steve and when things started going down, we were ready."

"What happened to him?" I ask.

"James or Steve?"

"James."

He's quiet for a long time, and I think I probably shouldn't have asked him.

"When we got here, the area wasn't clear. We split up. I thought I had my area clear. No, I *know* I had it clear. But a zombie came out of nowhere. James stepped in. Saved my life."

"Did he turn?"

"No."

I hug him tighter and I don't ask any more questions, because he's gulping and it looks like he's trying to breathe. He turns away, but I notice a tear on his face. I nestle into him and try to tell him it's okay, even when I know it's not.

I fall asleep with his arms tight around me.

Chapter 70

In the morning, we go right back to looking through the computers. I find an interesting thread, but I'm still about to bash my head against the desk from boredom when I feel a cool, wet nose against my leg. I look down and Sunshine wags her tail and licks me.

"Hey girl," I say and rub her head. "Hey, Sam, is there anywhere I can take Sunshine and throw a stick or something?"

He looks up, his gaze taking in me and the dog. "Hmmm. How about a picnic outside?"

"On the roof?"

"No. Outside for real."

"Sure."

So we grab some food, plates and drinks, put them in bags and then head to the Jeep. This time we pile into Sam's, with Cassie sitting in front and me and Sunshine in the back.

We emerge from the tunnel and it's like going

through a waterfall of sunlight. Everything's so bright. Sam takes us down a different path than what we came in on. It's a wooded lane with plenty of bumps which we take so fast it feels like the Jeep's hopping into the sky. Cassie gives a little squeal every time we hit air.

We tear around two corners in quick succession, one to the right and one to the left, and then we come out into a clearing rich with green grass about half the size of a football field. The clearing ends in a cliff with mountains visible in the distance. The sky is a perfect bright blue and filled with big, fluffy white clouds.

We pile out of the Jeep, and Sam and Cassie set up the picnic. I run to the edge of the woods to grab a stick and throw it for Sunshine. She runs full-out, passing the stick and then turning sharply to pick it up in her mouth and race back to me.

"Eww," I say, rubbing a bit of the slobber from the stick on my jeans. "Good girl. Get it!" I shout, and throw it again. She fetches it a couple more times and then it's time to eat. I sit down and plow into some chips and cold fried chicken.

"So, what have we all found out so far?" Sam asks.

Cassie grins. "I don't know what you guys have, but I found what I was looking for." She reaches into her pocket, pulls out a piece of paper and slaps it on the ground.

"We have a printer?" I ask.

"How long have you had that?" Sam asks.

"Yes." She answers me, then turns to Sam. "This morning before you guys even started."

"Then why did we keep looking?" I ask, thinking of the intense boredom of this morning.

"I wanted to be sure." She shrugs.

Sam gives her a dirty look, followed by one from me.

"So, what did you find?"

"It's an email between this guy and my dad. Apparently, they knew each other from some class they took together a long time ago. Anyways, at the start my dad wasn't even officially a part of the research. This guy asked my dad to look at this problem because they were such good friends and my dad was so good at everything.

"So he sent my dad his research, as well as some samples of the vaccine that weren't working. My dad didn't even get to start with infected blood – he started with a broken vaccine." She stabs the paper and sits back proudly.

"Why wouldn't they send him the infected blood?" I ask.

"They didn't want to let the blood out of the lab. In fact, my dad came here at one point."

"Did you find anything saying why they were involved with this at all?"

"The guy was a teacher here and worked part-time for the drug company, but that's all I found."

"Hmmm," I ponder.

"I might be able to help answer that," Sam says. We both look at him. "It's a drug company, right? What can you tell me about AIDS and a vaccine?"

"There isn't one," I respond.

"That's right." Sam points at me. "Instead, we have a list of drugs, some very expensive, that will keep you alive."

"Okay."

"What if the drug companies could create something like AIDS, scary as hell, but manageable with the right drugs, like AIDS?"

"That's horrible, Sam! And not very likely."

"Really? I've been going through the military side of things, right? They were originally included for military applications of a new drug and then they expanded it to a cleanup."

"I heard a lot of rumors after India that this was something created by the military," I tell them.

"I did, too, and it makes sense. But I came across this long email by the head of one of the divisions, talking about this great drug one of the other divisions was working on and how if it could be tweaked just a bit, the military would really like it. He was asking for marketing ideas for a drug that would create soldiers who couldn't feel pain, who would then create chaos in a region and then be 'reclaimed' when the job was finished."

"Reclaimed?" Cassie asks.

"Turned back to human with something like the vaccine, only different, right?" I try to understand.

Sam nods and I get a chill. It describes the zombies, all except for the part of reclaiming someone.

"Did they ever get the drug to turn someone back into human?" I ask.

"No." He shakes his head, dashing my hopes for ransacking the complex behind us for a cure.

"What did you find?" Cassie asks me.

"Nothing. Just a bunch of meeting notes and agendas."

"Oh, well." Cassie shoves her shoes off her feet and jumps up, grabbing the stick. "C'mon, Sunshine."

She runs off, waving the stick at the dog, back to being a kid again. I shake my head and grin at Sam. He looks at me suspiciously, then shrugs and runs after her.

I sit and finish my lunch, thinking. Sam was right to be suspicious of me. I just outright lied to both of them.

I *did* find something. I found evidence that someone tampered with Cassie's dad's results, deliberately shifting and mutating The Shot. Each batch was different, but pushed toward the same goal. It was all very hush-hush, directed by one of the executives of the company.

Each batch of The Shot was pushed and mutated and tested, all with one goal in mind. I finish my lunch and run off to play with Sunshine and my friends, with one phrase going round and round in my head.

'Sustainable immortality.'

Chapter 71

We toss the stick for Sunshine for a while before we change it to a form of tag. The humans have to tag a person with the stick, and that person throws it, and then whoever Sunshine brings the stick to is it and everything starts over. It sounds really complicated, but in the end it's just a bunch of running around, giggling and falling over.

Eventually I get tired and thirsty, and I go back to the picnic area and collapse on the blue blanket we've spread out. I grab a Coke and laugh as Sunshine brings the stick to Cassie for the third time in a row.

Sam joins me on the blanket, grabbing another soda out of the bag and cracking it open. He takes a good, long drink.

"I think Sunshine has chosen Cassie as her owner," he says.

"I think you're right," I agree, even though I'm a

bit disappointed. I like dogs, so it would have been neat if Sunshine thought I was hers. "Cassie does seem to spend a lot of time with her."

"Yeah." He takes another drink. "Look, I was thinking. Instead of you guys trying to find that compound north of us, how about you just stay here? There's a lab and everything."

There's this earnest, hopeful look in his eyes, like a puppy looks at you when you might take it home.

I think about the last few days and how fun it's been. How nice it's been to be safe. And yeah, I think about how much I like him. I smile.

"I'll talk about it with Cassie," I tell him. And this smile, this glorious, happy smile spreads across his face and his eyes glow. It's like watching somebody suddenly shine. I feel my smile grow wider.

And that's when the barking starts.

#

Sunshine's standing at the edge of the clearing, body ramrod straight, barking her tail off. Cassie runs toward Sunshine and I jump to my feet.

"This can't be good," I mutter and run toward them.

"No shit," Sam says behind me.

Cassie screams.

I don't remember hearing her scream before. My brave girl, screaming.

I put on an extra burst of speed even though I already feel a stitch forming. Cassie's gone beyond the edge of the clearing. She's gone into the woods and Sunshine's gone, too.

It seems like forever; time is slowing down, and what was a short distance of green stretches longer and longer.

Then, eventually, I reach the edge of the clearing and burst into the forest.

Cassie's there, beating the shit out of a zombie on the ground with a tree branch. No kidding.

"That's my girl," I say under my breath.

"Delilah, it was great, Sunshine totally jumped him and knocked him to the ground for me!" Cassie says, all in one breath.

"That's great," I respond, noticing there isn't any blood or anything on Sunshine - just in case. I don't think the virus has jumped to canines, but it's good to see the lack of a bite.

Then I hear it: a long, low zombie moan, followed by another and another.

Chapter 72

"Cassie," I whisper, holding my hand out.

A slow zombie in military fatigues ambles out of the brush and bumps into a tree. I see another behind him. The question is: how many are there? And are any of them fast zombies?

Then I hear crashing, like something moving very fast through the forest. That would be a yes.

"Cassie, run!" I shout. I grab her hand and start pulling as she looks over her shoulder.

"Sunshine, c'mon!" Cassie yells.

And then we're running, running as fast as we can for the Jeep.

"Run! Get the Jeep started!" I shout to a confused Sam as we get closer. I see him look past me and his mouth drop open, and then he pivots and races for the Jeep.

Dear God, why did we run so much before?

The stitch that had been forming in my side pops

instantly into place and I let go of Cassie's hand so she can run faster. At the last moment, I swerve to the side and swoop up her tennis shoes. I look behind me, and there's a young male zombie, in fatigues and without a shirt, running toward me like he's in an official race. He's not even moaning; it's just his fierce, determined eyes burning into me.

"Delilah!" Cassie shouts as I hear the Jeep roar to life.

I spin on my heel and sprint to the vehicle. Cassie and Sunshine make it in, and Cassie holds the door open for me. I throw the shoes behind her, grab the side to lift myself in and then slam the door shut. There's a thud against the back window; the male zombie's slammed full-throttle against the back, his hands flat against the glass.

"Go!" I shout.

The male's brown eyes stare right into mine, his eyes so focused, everything in him tense, alert and fierce. My throat goes dry as I realize I see no sign of biting. He's just like the babies: cracked skin but no wounds.

Then we take off, leaving him in our dust.

#

As we race back to the base, bumping along the way, I find myself staring out the window. Was that soldier – because that was what he was – deliberately infected?

Thinking about his lack of injuries, I bet he was.

Someone deliberately infected him, deliberately pushed and mutilated the work of Cassie's dad. Should I tell her? Should I tell her that everything he tried to do in his last days was changed and perverted just for one person's selfish goal?

Would it make her more determined to find a cure, or would it make her feel like crap? Would it hurt her?

The Jeep swerves around a corner and I grab one of the seats.

What about the person who did that? Is that executive out there somewhere infected? Is he still human, or did he reach his goal? Did he attain sustainable immortality, whatever that was?

Such an odd phrase, sustainable immortality. Wasn't that the point of immortality? Wasn't that the whole meaning?

Although, look at vampires. They were supposedly immortal, but they could still be killed with sunlight or a stake to the heart, right?

"That was a close call, wasn't it?"

"What?" I ask, jolted out of my thoughts.

"I said that was a close call, wasn't it?" Sam repeats.

"Definitely."

"Hey, how about when we get back we play video games?"

"Sure," I say. With effort, I shift my mind to the present. I forget about sustainable immortality, I forget about the soldier, and I ignore the fact that we almost died. I make the decision to focus on the two people in the car with me.

"How about a racing game?" I ask.

They both groan.

"You suck at those!" Cassie says.

"Yeah, but they're fun. And you don't have to kill anything."

"Okay." Sam shrugs.

"Okay." Cassie chimes in.

"Cool!" I say then bounce around like a bunny on the way in until Cassie dissolves into giggles and Sam looks at me like I'm crazy.

What the hey – I'll do anything for a laugh. And then I won't have to think.

Chapter 73

Later that night, I go into Cassie's bedroom. She likes to spend about half an hour playing PSP before she goes to sleep. I wave as I come in and shut the door, and she holds up a finger. I sit silently on the bed until she shuts it down.

"What's up?"

"I wanted to talk to you about something Sam brought up today."

"Okay." She raises her eyebrows and scoots back against the headboard.

"Sam asked if we want to stay here with him," I tell her and then just about hold my breath waiting for her response.

"But there aren't any adults here." She frowns.

"No, but we're safe here. We have plenty of food and we're not constantly running from zombies. Plus, there's a lab. Lots of labs."

Cassie crosses her arms. "Delilah, it's more than

being safe from zombies. I'm a kid. I'm supposed to have a mom and a dad."

"They're both gone, sweetie," I say as gently as I can.

"I know, but kids used to get adopted all the time. I know I won't ever get my real mom and dad back, but I still want parents. Somebody to take care of me."

"I thought we were doing that." I swallow.

"You're not a grown-up. What do you know how to cook? You don't read me stories. You left me alone for an entire morning. There isn't anybody to play with. You're off with Sam and it's just me."

"I can play with you more often."

"It's not just that. I want a mom."

"I thought we were taking care of you okay," I respond, as tears slip down my face even though I don't want them to. I wipe them roughly and quickly away.

Cassie hugs me. "I know you're trying real hard, but you're not a mom. You're not a little kid, but you're still a kid, too. It's okay." She pats my back.

I hug her, too. I didn't realize she felt this way, but it makes sense. I'm older than her. I miss my mom, but really I've enjoyed the freedom and I've enjoyed making decisions on my own.

"I didn't know," I say over Cassie's shoulder. "We'll find you someone."

"Thanks, Delilah." She pats my back again.

We both calm down, and I tuck her in and shut the door behind me. It's at that point that I realize I told her we would find *her* someone, not that we would find *us* someone.

#

I go into the living room and find Sam still playing video games. He pauses the game when I sit down on the couch.

"What'd she say?"

"How did you know I talked to her?" I smile.

He shrugs. "Just assumed. So?"

My smile slips away. "She really wants a mom and dad."

He looks at the TV. "We're all orphans now. We're on our own."

"She really wants adults," I say quietly.

"Yeah, okay." He shrugs again, but this time it's a quick up and down movement, as if tossing something off his back. He avoids my gaze. "And you?"

"What do you mean, and me?"

Sam puts down the controller and looks right at me. "Do you want to stay?"

Chapter 74

"Yes, of course, but Cassie doesn't."

"No, I mean, will you stay without Cassie?"

"Oh," I say as I realize what he's asking. And a weird thing happens: I feel warm all over, but a lump forms in my throat, too. "I don't know," I reply, just surprised and thrilled all at the same time.

"It's okay. Just forget it." He puts the controller on the floor and I touch his arm.

"No. You asked. Just let me think for a bit. I promised some things to Cassie before you and I even met."

He stops getting up and just looks at me really intensely, like he's trying to figure out something from my expression.

"I like Cassie, but I like you, too." I raise my hands, not sure what to do or say to get him to believe me, to get him to understand that I'm hesitating because of my friendship with Cassie, not because I don't like him. *Crap, this stuff is confusing.* I quickly hug him and pat him on the back then go get a Coke.

The next morning, I find Sam sitting at the table with printouts spread before him. He looks bleak.

"Is Cassie awake?" he asks.

"I think so. I'll go get her," I say, concerned by Sam's behavior. I return with Cassie and we both sit down as he gives us each a piece of paper.

"I've found the compound that's north of Denver."

I look down at my paper. It's a picture taken from the air of a small town that's been walled in.

"They must have started building the wall as soon as the virus hit American shores," Sam states.

"That was quite a leap," I say. "A lot of people thought we could stop it."

"Maybe they were playing it safe." He shrugs.

"Any sign of any kids?" Cassie's on her knees in her chair so she can lean over the table.

"No." Sam shakes his head. "But they could still be there."

"Sign of adults? Sign of healthy people?" I ask.

"Yes. Also some signs of gardens and livestock."

"Almost like they were ready?"

"More like they're getting ready for winter. There were farms in the area before, so I'm guessing they just nabbed some dairy cows."

I lean back, watching Sam. It's like he's just shut himself off. I glance at Cassie and she's so immersed in the picture she doesn't even notice.

I know why he's closed himself off. To find this so soon after we found out how Cassie felt...

I'm sad, too. I want to stay. I want to stay with Sam and with Cassie. I don't understand why this has to change, but seeing the excitement on Cassie's face I'm pretty sure she's not changing her mind about leaving.

This means I'm going to have to choose.

Crap.

Abandon my best friend with strangers, or leave my new, hot friend alone? Somebody I care about, too. This really sucks.

"How far away is it?" I ask.

"In the old days, about three to four hours depending on traffic. Now? I'm not sure. Probably one to three days."

"Well?" I turn to Cassie.

She grins at me. "When can we go?"

"How about we pack the Jeep today and head out tomorrow?" Sam says.

I feel like someone hit me in the chest with a hammer.

"Great!" Cassie jumps up. "Woo-hoo!" She exclaims, and then bounces out of the room headed toward her stuff.

I reach across the table and grab his hand. I love the slightly rough texture and I love the warmth.

"Stay," he says.

"Come with us," I tell him at about the same time.

"I'll come with you during the trip. I'll take you guys there." His thumb rubs the top of my hand. "But Delilah…" He leans over the table and kisses me. "Please come back with me."

"We'll think of something," I placate him. And then for once, I do something physical I actually want to do, without hesitating. I crawl into his lap, put my head on his shoulder and hug him, and I let him hold me.

Chapter 75

We have Sam's Jeep packed by that afternoon. We're taking just his vehicle because if we stay then we won't need one anymore. I don't like it – I really like having my own car – but I want to spend more time with Sam. And I figure I can take another one any time I want.

Sam gives Cassie a laptop and a solar charger, which is really nice of him. We spend the afternoon playing video games. I go off for a bit to try and take a nap, but wind up just tossing and turning, thinking about the whole Cassie-Sam problem. I'm in bed, just about to give up when there's a knock on the door.

"Yeah?" I open it and sit on the bed. Cassie's standing in the doorway with something hidden behind her back and she has a huge smile on her face.

"What?" I ask.

She swishes back and forth, and then finally

brings my long, black skirt from behind her, only now it's decorated with flowers.

I'm torn because she took a skirt I really like, but on the other hand the flowers look pretty.

"Thank you, Cassie! Where did you get the flowers?"

"They were growing between this building and the next."

Did I mention they're all sunflowers? I'm not fond of sunflowers, but heck, real flowers are nothing to sneeze at these days.

"You're not supposed to go out there alone!"

"I wasn't alone. Sam came with me."

"Why?"

"You'll see. Now, put on your skirt!" She jumps up and down. "And a white top!"

I comply, even though I'm a bit suspicious. Cassie climbs on the bed and fixes my hair.

"Wait there!" she says and runs off. She comes back a few seconds later, taking a running leap onto the bed.

"Okay," she says breathlessly, and puts some sort of yellow paper on my head.

"What is it?" I take it off.

"Ohh, now you messed up your hair," she pouts.

It's a paper crown; basically a strip of paper stapled together. It's been colored with yellow highlighter so it looks gold and there's a butterfly sticker, a gold star and a strawberry sticker.

"Do you like the stickers? I found them in my bag." Cassie fixes my hair and puts the crown back on.

"I do. The butterfly's very pretty. Are we playing princess or something?"

"Nope." She grins.

"You're up to something." I squint and point at her, trying not to laugh.

"Uh-huh." She takes my hand and leads me out to the elevator and up to the roof. We go through the door and I just stop.

"It's beautiful," I breathe.

There are white emergency candles lit everywhere. Paper chains, colored with yellow highlighter, are strung up. Ahead of me is what used to be the picnic table, only now it's covered in a sheet, with two plates and sunflowers in a glass on top.

"Oh, very cool, Cassie," I say. Then Sam steps from the side with a sunflower in his hand. He's wearing black jeans, a black t-shirt, and a paper crown colored with yellow highlighter. He smiles at me, and then I hear Cassie behind me start some music.

"Welcome to the Zombie Base Dance," she says, and then closes the door behind her, leaving me alone with Sam.

Chapter 76

"Hi," I say.

"Hey." He hands me the sunflower and kisses me. He leads me over to the table, has me sit, and then changes the music.

"Hey, I recognize that!" I say as Lady Gaga starts singing.

"Yep." He grins. "We grabbed it from your phone."

"Thanks."

Sam piles chicken nuggets and mac'n'cheese on my plate.

"Sorry, it's not exactly a steak dinner. I wanted spaghetti – like that Disney movie – but we didn't have any." He sits down after filling his plate.

"It's perfect," I remark.

We crack open sodas and start eating. We talk about lighter things, happier things while we eat, and we smile and laugh together. We finish around the same time, and Sam changes the music to "Umbrella". He walks back to me and extends his hand.

"Can I have this dance?"

"Sure." I slip my arms around my neck, he puts his arms around my waist, and we do that shuffle-shuffle thing that is slow-dancing.

Sam pulls back from me a bit. "You're really amazing, you know that? You're fun and you're beautiful." He strokes my hair.

"Thank you. You, too," I reply.

"I'm serious," he says, and then he kisses me again. I feel warm all over, and then he hugs me to him.

I close my eyes and breathe in his scent, feel the warm air, and listen to the music as we do that soft, slow turn.

I want to remember every moment.

I have this feeling, this tickling feeling deep in my stomach, that this might be my last moment of peace for a while.

#

The next morning, we head out with me in the front passenger seat and Cassie and Sunshine in the back. As we leave the parking area, though, Sam makes a turn instead of going straight.

"Hey, we're not going out?"

"We are. But this way puts us right on the valley and then it's a straight shot to the road we need."

"Oh, okay." I shrug. We race through a dimly lit tunnel made of concrete. Every few feet, yellow lights high on the wall flash by. Eventually Sam jolts to a stop, but fortunately the seat belt holds me in place. The gate opens and we drive through into the bright, sunlit world.

The door shuts behind us just as something hits the car, which is quickly followed by another hit, and then another. A scream starts to build and leaks out a bit before I clamp a hand over my mouth.

We're surrounded by zombies.

Chapter 77

Sam honks the horn and I look at him incredulously.

"That's not going to work. They don't care about noise."

"Some of the fast ones do," he clarifies.

"Huh."

And he's right; some of them step out of the way, as if out of habit. Unfortunately, some of the slow ones amble in.

"Oh, well." Sam shrugs and revs the engine. "We'll have to do it the fun way, I guess."

He grins and the Jeep leaps forward as I grab the bar near my head. Bodies fall from sight, and the vehicle climbs. We're still walled in on the sides, though, and unfortunately I left my window partially unrolled. I don't notice that fact until I feel something in my hair. I reach up absentmindedly to bat at it, and I touch something cold. I look up at that point to see a zombie staring at me through the glass, its hand over the windows and its fingers digging into my scalp.

I scream as those cold fingers wrap around my hair and yank.

"Shit," Sam swears. The Jeep swings wildly in a circle but the damn zombie still hangs on, ripping out my hair as we go.

Desperately I dig into the bag at my feet, trying to ignore the pain from my head as my hands touch metal. I grab the gun, brace as Sam takes another turn, click the safety off and position the gun point-blank where the zombie's head is.

"Look away!" I shout.

"Don't shoot!" Sam says.

"What?!"

"Don't shoot! We need that window!" Sam says.

"What the fuck do you want me to do then?" I screech as the zombie's icky wet hands curl in my hair.

"Roll up the window!" he shouts.

Dammit. I drop the gun and grab the thing's fingers. God, touching them is even worse than them touching me. They're wet, and I really hope I don't have any cuts that its blood can seep into.

I force the fingers up and the empty-head fights me. Eventually, I get them out of the window and roll it up quickly.

I collapse back against the seat and breathe

heavily, even with the zombie's black eyes still starting at me and its mouth opening and closing against the glass. Then I see it move and hear a bong against the side of the Jeep.

"It's on the roof," Cassie states.

"That works," Sam says. He speeds up and then hits the brakes, hard. The male goes flying and lands in the grass ahead of us. Sam leisurely turns us away.

It's at that point that I notice that in the middle of all this, Sam got us free of the rest of the zombies. I hit him on the shoulder for good measure.

"What's that for?"

"For driving into a pile of zombies. Why'd we have to go that way?"

"It was clear last night."

"So, what the hell happened?"

"Look!" Cassie points between our seats. We've gone over a hill, and yep, there's the answer right there.

Maybe half a mile in front of us is the smoldering remains of an SUV.

Chapter 78

We coast to a stop, staring at what's left of the vehicle.

"How long ago?" I ask.

"It wasn't there last night. I'm not seeing any flames, but it's definitely still hot. I don't know, maybe an hour or so? Maybe more? Definitely since last night at midnight."

The doors of the SUV are torn open. The only bit of color left on the vehicle is near the back, and it's a dark blue. There's a brown backpack on the ground and a blue blanket caught on one of the back doors, fluttering in the breeze.

"Are they still alive?" Cassie asks.

"I don't know, honey."

Dear God, if we'd left an hour ago, two hours ago, would we have found them still alive? What was I doing two hours ago? If we'd just gotten up a bit earlier...

"Maybe they're still around." Cassie lunges to the other side of the Jeep and looks out the window.

"They're not," Sam says quietly.

"You don't know that!"

"You're right; I don't. But they would have had to leave the car, and there are zombies all around here."

"Crap," I mutter. Five minutes? If we'd left five minutes earlier, would we have found them, helped them?

Sam sighs. "Okay. Tell you what. I'll drive away from the zombies, and away from the car, but kind of slow. Keep an eye for anything that might be them. Maybe they got lucky, maybe they found a rock somewhere."

I love him for that. I love him for looking.

But even though we drive slowly for half an hour, we don't find anything.

#

We've been driving for a couple of hours when Sam slows to a crawl.

"Oh, God," he whispers.

"What?" Cassie grabs the edge of my seat and peers around.

"I heard it was bad," I say, looking ahead. "I just didn't expect it to be this bad."

"Yeah."

"But didn't you see it on the way down?" I ask Sam.

"Naw, we went through the mountains."

Denver. It had been a beautiful city, especially from the footage I saw of the 2008 political convention.

It was just awful, what had happened here.

My eyes flit over the destruction, the ruin, refusing to see it all.

We're silent for a few minutes. I just keep thinking about those poor people. I want to see it how it used to be, even though there isn't even anyone left to rebuild it. There's no one left to say, 'not only can we rebuild, but we can make it better'.

I stab at my eyes, willing the tears not to fall. We may not be able to build a great and shining city again in my lifetime. But dammit, I want to build something pretty and good and better, even if it's something small.

Sunshine pushes her wet nose into my hand and whines. I hug her, and realize I've been gripping my shamrock and USB drive.

"It's okay, girl. C'mon guys; let's go," I say softly.

"Yeah," Cassie agrees. "We've got work to do."

#

We drive the rest of the day, even though sometimes it seems like we're not getting very far because we have to keep taking detours. The route Sam takes is a good one, though, because we hardly see any zombies. A lot of wreckage, but few zombies.

The sun is bright, the sky is blue, and we have each other.

We settle down for the night in a barn, with doors that will still close. We don't light a fire for dinner, so we have cold pork'n'beans, some bread, and some cold leftover hot dogs. We sing 'Home on the Range' until Sunshine howls and Cassie collapses into giggles, and then we're off to bed in the Jeep, just in case.

I feel like I'm holding my breath, even though I'm not.

Chapter 79

I wake up in the middle of the night. I don't think I was screaming or anything because Sam, Cassie and Sunshine are all still asleep. I stare out into the utter darkness of the barn and remember some vague dream about my mom.

It hits me then. The last time I headed out into this world with someone I loved, she died. She died, and it was my fault...

The TV and the phones hadn't worked for a week. I mean, we could still turn them on, but you couldn't connect a call, and nothing came through on the television. Mom was determined to head to California and find Dad and Mike. Dad had been demanding that we stay where we were the last time we'd talked with him. He didn't think it was safe for anybody to go anywhere. No going to get them, and they weren't coming to get us.

My mom decided he was wrong, decreed that we

were going to go find them. She'd always stop abruptly at that point: just go find them. But both of us could fill out the rest of the sentence; go find them and be a family again. Mom and I agreed on that, even though I wasn't holding my breath anymore.

As much as it hurt, I didn't think they truly wanted us anymore, zombies or not.

I didn't want to go because I didn't want to leave the house. I kept insisting they would get through on the phone, that landlines were better than cell phones, so we'd hear from them if we just stayed. But looking back on it now, I know the truth. I was terrified. I was scared of leaving the house, not to mention going across half the country.

It was just scary, and I couldn't face it.

I threw a temper tantrum when Mom insisted we go. I caused a fight and then hid in my room. She packed the entire car herself, alone, even though it was very dangerous at that point. And when she finally came to me, she had to practically drag me out of the house kicking and screaming.

So we're there by the car, and I was screaming and arguing and crying. I kept claiming they would call in the next few minutes, and if we could just go inside she would see that. I was making a hell of a racket. My mom had me by the arm and was insisting I get in the car. I wrenched myself out of her grasp and turned to go into the house.

A zombie was right there.

He was covered in blood and his clothes were torn. He opened his mouth and moaned.

We both shut up instantly, tears still streaming down my face, my mouth open. The zombie seemed a bit surprised by the lack of noise, and then he came at me.

I froze.

Mom rushed past me and tackled him. They hit the ground hard, and then he overpowered her and I heard her scream.

There were other zombies then, and Celie came out of nowhere and hit them with a bat. She grabbed my hand and then we were out of there, leaving the door to my house open and the car loaded and my mom... my mom still on the ground.

It was all my fault and I stood idly by.

#

So now, I look at these two people I love – yes, love – and wonder how on Earth can I lead them out into this world? How can I say to them that I am someone safe to travel with? How can I tell them that they can count on me?

Chapter 80

The next day, we'd been traveling for a few hours when we hit the edge of a small town. I look for zombies but all I see are abandoned cars, open houses and blood. Then we drive past a nice little park, complete with an overgrown green lawn.

"Stop!" Cassie calls out.

"Why?" I ask.

"Look!" She points, and then I see movement near one of the trees in the middle of the park. It's a man – an adult – and I think he sees us.

"Is he a zombie?" Sam asks.

"I don't think so."

The guy stops and waves his arms while jumping up and down.

"Nope, not a zombie," I state. I roll down the window and shout out, "C'mon!"

The man runs toward us. I think he's in his late-thirties. He's balding but trying to hide it with his hair cut short and spiky. He's wearing khakis, sneakers, and a torn red polo shirt.

"What's that sound?" Cassie asks.

"Oh my God," Sam murmurs.

"What?" I question, looking at where he's pointing. The sound is a low rumble of zombie moans, and I'd say there are at least a hundred, a lot of them fast, pouring through the park.

"Run!" I shout.

The guy doesn't even look over his shoulder, just pumps his arms and pushes his head down. Cassie opens her door and scoots over to the other side and holds Sunshine. He leaps into the Jeep, saying "Ow" at the same time. He pulls the door shut behind him.

"Floor it!" he shouts. "Straight ahead!" The fast zombies are maybe two blocks behind him. The man rolls down the window and screams out, "Fuck you! Fuck you!"

In the mirror, I see him raise something black, something that looks like a remote for a TV, and then press it triumphantly. First I hear a sound, a pow, followed by a rumble, and then something explodes on the other side of the park. Sam floors it and the Jeep jumps forward. The guy, the adult, is laughing as buildings explode all around town.

Finally, he calms down and rolls up the window.

He looks at us, and we look at him. I'm sure my eyes are as wide as saucers. He's dirty and there are tracks in his skin from sweat, but it's been ages since I've seen anyone as gloriously happy as this guy is at this minute.

"I got 'em, man. I got 'em," he mumbles to himself and then seems to notice where we are. "Take a left here."

Sam complies and I grab for the bar above my head as we swing around the corner.

"Kids, huh?" The guy nods a couple of times as if it makes complete sense. "Hey, take a right here, buddy, and stop, okay?" He slaps the side of Sam's seat, like I've seen other men slap each other's backs.

We turn around the corner and there's a black SUV sitting there alone under a tree.

"Hey, great job, buddy. Good luck, okay!" And with a smile and a wave, he's out the door and trotting to his vehicle. We watch him get in and drive off in stunned silence.

"Adults are crazy," Sam states. He turns in his seat and looks at Cassie. "You sure you want to go to this compound full of them?"

"Yeah," she says, but she doesn't sound as sure as a few hours ago.

Chapter 81

It's still daylight when Sam suggests pulling over for the night.

"Isn't it a little early?" Cassie asks.

"Yeah, but this way we get a good night's sleep and show up at the compound rested and looking good," Sam explains.

We all agree, but I think he just wants another night with us. That's cool with me; I'd like another night with him.

We're in the country, surrounded by hills and fields of gently waving grass. Some of the hills are rather large, and at the top of one we find hay baled into squares, stacked four high and three wide.

"Probably kept out here to feed cattle," Sam says.

"That makes sense," I concur.

"So, we're sleeping in the Jeep again?" Cassie asks with a sour face.

"Nope, we're sleeping up there." Sam points to

the top of the hay stack.

"Really?"

"Yeah." He smiles. "Just put down some blankets and we'll be fine."

There's no place we want to really light a fire, so we break out some bread, canned peaches and Vienna sausages.

"I don't really like these sausages," Sam complains.

"Better than sardines," I tell him.

"Yeah." He shrugs. "I could still use a steak."

"Me, too. How about you, Cassie?"

"I'd love a pizza!"

"That sounds good." I toss Sunshine a sausage and she swallows it whole.

After dinner, Sam shows Cassie how to carefully climb the hay, and then she starts setting up our sleeping area.

Sam and I hold hands and walk over to another haystack nearby. As soon as we're out of sight, he pulls me into his arms and kisses me.

I lose everything but him for a few minutes, and when we eventually stop I'm thankful to find that no zombies sneaked up on us. I'm pressed back against the hay, and there's this wonderful green scent coming from it.

"Let's take her there, make sure she's safe, and then go home. We can come visit her every once in a while."

"Why don't you just stay there with us?"

He kisses me again and it feels like he's pressuring me with his kisses. It's like he's saying, 'stay with me' when he does it.

I break off the kiss so I can hug him.

"I don't understand why you won't at least try it."

"Exactly. I don't understand why you won't, either." I put my head on his shoulder but that just makes it worse. My whole body lights up. I rack my brain trying to think of something, of some way for this to work. Why can't I just have both?

"I want to be with you." He hugs me tighter. His scent, his touch, makes it so much harder to think.

"I want to be with you, too," I admit. And then I let everything go, so I can just enjoy the present, enjoy him. Then I kiss him.

After we come back, we tie a rope around Sunshine and lift her up on the haystack. She sniffs every edge but fortunately doesn't fall off. Then we all settle down and go to sleep with all of us snuggled near each other. I feel safe, warm and happy. Then I drift off to sleep.

In the morning, I wake up and I'm the only one left on the stack. The blankets are crumbled and just left behind.

Then I hear shouting.

I scramble to the edge of the hay, my heart pounding in my chest. I don't have any weapons on me. I peer over the edge, fearing the worst, but I don't see any zombies. Instead, Sam and Cassie are yelling at each other.

"She's staying with me!" Cassie shouts.

"No! She told me last night she's going to be with me!"

Oh, crap. He totally misunderstood what I said.

"Cassie! Sam!" I shout and scramble down, but by the time I make it to the ground both of them are headed in different directions.

"Cassie! Sam!" I yell again, but neither of them turns around. I sink to the ground and pull my knees in against my chest.

Crap. How have I made things even worse?

Chapter 82

God, Sam thought last night that I'd finally agreed to stay with him, even though that wasn't really what I meant.

Okay, I've got to come up with an answer before they come back and it's got to be good. But I can't leave Cassie. She's all alone in this world, and she's too young to look after herself. What if she winds up with a bad new parent? Will she know what to do? Who will protect her, look after her?

But I want to be with Sam. I've never felt this way for anyone else. He sits near me and I feel like I'm vibrating inside. He's such a cool person, too. I want to know him better.

I don't know why he's being so stubborn about this. Really, how hard is it going to be to live with adults again? We can just ignore the stuff we don't like. Sure, they'll punish us, but really, what can they do?

Okay, so then every bad, abusive scene from a movie pops in my head. And with the zombies they can get pretty creative, and there aren't any cops to help out anymore, either.

But what if they thought we were adults somehow? I mean, okay, with me it's stretching it a bit, but Sam isn't so far off. What if we say he's older, say eighteen, and we say I'm a bit younger than him?

But if we say I'm under eighteen, they could still separate us, right? They could say I need a guardian, or a stepmom or whatever, and she could say I can't see him anymore.

That's bullshit!

Okay, maybe I see a bit of what he's saying about adults. I don't want to go back to that either. I mean, I can take care of myself.

And then I think of something, something where they would have to treat us like grown-ups.

We could tell them we're married.

Yeah, we could do that. We could say our parents were worried about us being all alone if something bad happened with the zombies and let us get married.

That would work, right? Nobody orders around married people. We could live together and do what we want.

Yes! Now, I've just got to convince Sam.

I smile to myself and then get everything piled

back into the Jeep, ready for when the others come back.

Hours go by.

#

The sun's beating down on me and I'm worried all to hell. I bet it's noon by now and neither of them have returned. I pace back and forth, trying to choose a direction. Should I go after Cassie? She's little, but she also has Sunshine. Should I go after Sam? Did he take a weapon?

Crap!

Then I hear a shout.

"Delilah!"

It's Sam. I jump up, happy to hear him.

"Yeah?" I yell back. "Hey, Sam, I know how to fix everything." I run toward his voice, near the edge of the hill. "Let's just tell them we're married!"

"Delilah!" And it's this horrible, ragged cry. For a minute, I think that means he doesn't want to tell people he's married to me. Then the sound of it sinks in.

His voice is full of sorrow and pain.

Chapter 83

He comes over the top of the hill and I freeze.

Sam's covered in blood. His shirt's torn and his hair's messed up. And his leg... His leg's been mangled.

Tears slide down my cheeks.

"Delilah," he says softly.

"Please, tell me it was a dog," I practically beg.

"Can't." He collapses to the ground.

I scream. I don't care if the damn zombies come. I scream and I shout "No!" over and over.

He lays there in a little heap, like he feels really bad. And I realize that what I'm doing isn't helping at all. The tears stream down my face and I do everything I can to pull myself together, to calm down long enough to help a bit.

I kneel on the ground and pull him into my arms, and he makes a long, low pained sound.

"Are you hurt inside?"

"No, not like you mean. Just the virus."

There are streaks of sweat down his face. God, if I'd gone out earlier I could have helped him, could have eased his pain, even just a bit.

"What happened?"

I carefully shift so his head's in my lap. He snuggles into me, even though I can tell it hurts. Sam closes his eyes for a minute, and then opens his beautiful, green eyes to stare off into the horizon.

"The Jeep's fucked. So after the fight, I went to get oil. I'd noticed a convenience store a bit before we pulled over last night. Thought that was worth a try.

"I was in the store, looking for the oil, when it bit my leg. You just don't expect them to go straight for your leg, you know? You don't expect them to crawl on the floor. But that's what it did. Just crawled right up and took a chunk out of me.

"I put five bullets in it and it almost reached my neck before it finally stopped. By then, it was too late. It took me hours to get back here."

I'm not going to stop the crying; it's all I can do to keep breathing normally. I stroke his hair and he pushes his head into my hand.

"I'm sorry I didn't come find you."

"It's okay." He looks up at me. "You would really tell people you're married to me?"

"Yeah." And a smile spreads across my face at the thought, even from under all the tears.

He smiles then and it's his glorious, happy smile. He leans up, even after wincing from the pain, and we kiss.

It's the best kiss I've ever had. He reaches up and we hold hands. Carefully, I break off the kiss and then slide down, so we're holding each other.

Then I think of something. I search both his wrists, slide my hands up higher.

"Are you just not wearing the bracelet? When did you get it?"

"Get what?"

"The Shot. When did you get The Shot?" My mind races through the months, trying to remember from the memos which batches were the strongest. Obviously, the later he got his the better the chance we have.

"I didn't get it."

"What?!" I stop my frantic search and stare at him.

"I didn't get it, Delilah," he says gently. "Too broke. Nobody cared. Nobody ever cared, except you."

He kisses me again, even as the tears flow faster and faster. We wrap ourselves around each other. Then he breaks off the kiss and holds my face. He strokes my hair with the other hand and looks straight into my eyes.

"Come with me, Delilah," he pleads.

"What?" I ask, surprised.

"Come with me, just like Sid and Nancy."

I don't know what's on my face at this moment, but my heart's beating like a drum.

"They didn't get to die together at the same time, but then they still got to be together. If we die near the same time, we'll get to be together."

"But we won't be dead."

"No, see, that's even better. I've seen them, Delilah. I've seen the zombies that still hold on to each other. We could be like that. Together, until Cassie finds the cure."

And then he kisses me again.

My heart's pounding out of my chest.

I don't want to die.

What he's saying is very romantic, very sweet. Yes, I would like to spend the rest of my life with him, but I don't want to die.

"I'm afraid." It slips out and I didn't even mean to say anything.

"Me, too," he admits. "But we'll be together. It'll be okay."

And it will leave Cassie all alone in the world.

I pull back and look at him. His eyes are warm and so full of love. He really does want to be with me.

"I love you," I say, and I really mean it.

"I love you, too." That glorious smile breaks over

his face like a sunrise, and he kisses me and then holds me close.

I close my eyes and breathe him in, feeling his chest rise and fall. He's so warm against me. Then he stiffens.

"No," I moan, and tears start falling again.

"It's okay." He pats me as best as he can, and then he tenses again, pulling away from me in pain. He turns so his back is on the ground then rises a bit from the pain, his hands clenching and opening. I grab his hand and find his skin is burning hot.

His eyes catch mine.

"I love you," he repeats. Then he gives out a long, low moan and goes still.

His hand is still warm in mine but his eyes are closed, and I lose it.

I get up and walk a few steps away, turning my back to him. I cry and I make those horrible sounds like my mom made. I finally understand why she made them, what it took to wrench them out of her.

God, this hurts. This hurts so much. I want him back now.

I turn and look at him.

Maybe I should have gone with him.

"Delilah?" A little girl's voice calls out.

"Cassie?"

I wipe my tears away, trying to see, when Cassie comes over the hill. It's at that point that the zombie that is Sam opens his eyes and moans.

He moves, and that's when I realize he is between me and Cassie. He's closer to her.

Cassie screams.

Chapter 84

He's seen her. Dear God, he's seen her.

"No, not her," I plead. "Not her, too." My hands clench into fists and I run.

He lunges.

I build up speed as fast as I can, tensing every part of my body. He misses her the first time and goes for her again, but then I'm there and I leap at him.

I put my hands out and tackle him. It's as we're flying through the air that the thought whizzes through my brain that this is how my mom died.

And then we hit the ground and roll. There's a sharp pain in my neck and another one in my side, and then I'm on my back stiff-arming him away from me.

"Stop it, Sam," I demand, even though I know it's not really him. Sick fear runs through me. He's so much stronger than me. This isn't going to last long.

This is how my mom died, this is how my mom died, this is how my mom died...

"Hey, Sam," Cassie calls out.

We both look – God knows why he does – and then she swings a shovel just like I taught her and bangs him on the head.

It's enough to get him off me. I jump up, the panic and adrenaline still pumping through me and making my hands shake. I put one hand out for the shovel and she gives it to me.

"Sorry, Sam," I say, and give him a good hit on the head. He hits the ground and stops moving.

Cassie and I look at him.

"I don't think you've killed him," she tells me.

"Me, neither." I drop the shovel and grab his arms. God, he's heavy.

"Get your backpack out of the Jeep and mine, too," I instruct. Cassie runs ahead of me, Sunshine nipping at her heels.

I drag him over to the Jeep while Cassie throws out supplies, and then runs around and opens the driver's door. I boost and shove him in there as best as I can. It's not pretty and he'd be hurting if he was still human, but it works. I slam the door shut.

"Wait for the cure, Sam." I put my hand on the driver's door window.

"How are we going to use the Jeep now?" Cassie asks.

"We're not. He told me it was fucked before he died."

I watch him for a few moments, not wanting to move away yet, and then I see him wake up. There's a moment where he seems himself, and then he sees me and throws himself at the window, his mouth open and his eyes crazed.

"I love you," I whisper, and take my hand away from the Jeep and step back. "We'll come back for you."

I turn and find Cassie holding a shirt in her hand and crying.

"I know. I'm sad, too, honey. But it'll be okay."

She shakes her head and motions me closer. She gets up on her tippy toes and holds the shirt against my neck. It stings. And then I realize my neck feels wet.

I pull the shirt away from my neck and it's covered in blood.

Cassie's crying gets louder as I hold the shirt in my hand and sink to the ground.

"Oh, God." It's all I can think to say.

Chapter 85

I've been afraid of becoming a zombie this whole time. Everyone is, of course, but now I will become one for sure. I sit with the blood from the shirt cooling on my hands and I realize I will die but not *die*. I will become –

I shut my eyes and force everything out. There is one last thing I must do. I have to get Cassie to safety.

I put the shirt on the ground and stand up.

"Come on. We need to get to the compound."

Cassie just looks at me, crying and shaking her head. I make sure there's no blood on my hands and then I kneel down and gently touch her sleeves.

"We need to get you somewhere safe. Now."

She nods and then collapses into more tears. Sunshine comes over and pushes her nose into Cassie's hand. She hugs the dog tightly, and I'm glad Sunshine's able to give her a hug when I can't.

Emotionally, I feel cold inside, just cut off, with

the thought of getting Cassie safely to the compound before I turn pounding in my head.

I get up and grab a bottle of water. I scrub my hands and neck until they're clean of blood. I take one of my shirts, tear off a strip and tie it around my neck, in a way I hope looks like a nifty scarf. I double-check that I'm clean of blood then walk over and gently touch Cassie's arm.

She looks me over and then throws herself at me, wrapping her arms around me so tightly that I can't breathe for a bit.

I sit on the ground, and that's when we both dissolve into tears.

It's a good cry. I feel like I should have done this long ago. But as it ends and we both quiet down, I can just feel a bit of the pain from the virus spreading through me. It's a dull ache at this point, but I know it's a sign.

We get up and head out with Cassie's hand in mine.

#

We walk for a long time. The pain spreads slowly, building bit by bit, just like the flu. It reminds me a bit of a mix of food poisoning and flu, actually. It feels like you've been poisoned, and it feels serious.

I worry that we won't make it there in time.

"How long does it take?" I ask.

"It's different for everyone. Longer if you took The Shot."

"I did."

And now I'm back to thinking about The Shot. It took us so long to get the money. I got the last batch available before everything shut down. I let that thought ping-pong through my mind and then I close it off. I can't have hope; not for my sake, and not for Cassie's. Better not to have hope and then have it wrenched away.

I don't want her to see me turn. I don't want her to see me at the end, in all that pain.

I pick up the pace a bit, and then eventually we come up over a hill. There, on the other side, is the compound.

Chapter 86

From above, I can see that the compound is really a small town surrounded by a metal fence. Even with a nice, green lawn around it, it's tiny; maybe a thirty-minute walk from one side to the other if you walk slowly. There's a portion near the northeast section where they're building a cement wall, but it's definitely a work in progress. Good idea, though. Get the temporary measure put in then create the permanent structure.

I kind of expected a lot of zombies around the place, but I don't see any in sight. I spot the entrance to the northwest and we head down.

When we get close the entrance – about a football field away – we hear a gunshot. Cassie and I stop still and hold up our hands.

"Stop there!" A voice shouts out over a megaphone. I glance at Cassie and she shrugs.

"If you're still human, follow the path between

the stones to the front gate. DO NOT stray outside of the path."

"Very fairy book," Cassie mutters.

"Yeah, right."

We carefully wind down a nice, white graveled path bordered on both sides by gray rocks. In some spots, I notice blood and torn grass.

"I think they might have set up a minefield around the town," I say.

"Makes sense," Cassie responds.

"Just be very careful if you ever have to leave in a hurry."

"Yes, Mooommm." Cassie rolls her eyes. I grin back at her and push her shoulder a bit. She shoves herself into me and I stumble, and we both giggle a bit.

We reach the front gate and our smiles fade. It was good to have one more bit of fun, but this is it. This is goodbye. Tears form in my eyes.

We're standing in front of a metal gate. Behind that is a small, fenced area consisting of just grass, and behind that is another fenced gate followed by a door.

A short, balding man wrenches open the door. He's wearing khakis and a striped shirt, and looks a bit harassed. He takes one look at us and calls over his shoulder, "Ferals!"

"Ferals?! What the –"

I put up a hand and stop Cassie in mid-speech. "What're you talking about, mister?"

Just then a big, round woman pushes him out of the way. "Shut up, Larry. The kids are okay."

"You haven't even seen them yet, Glenda."

And then I realize what he's talking about. He's calling us feral. Why? Just because we're kids?

"He doesn't mean any harm. Not all the kids who have come here are okay in the head. But you are, aren't you, honey?"

The woman swoons over Cassie like she's a dog. She opens the gate and pulls Cassie straight into a bear hug. Sunshine follows with a half-hearted wag of her tail and a whine.

"Glenda, you can't do that. They have to go into quarantine. They could be infected."

"She's not infected." I point at Cassie. "I am. I'm not coming inside." I put my hands up and try to look harmless.

The woman gasps and pulls Cassie back with her. I roll my eyes. Then I notice Cassie's backpack is still on my side. I hold it up.

"She needs her backpack."

Glenda looks at me like I've lost my mind.

"Please?" I look at Larry. "And could I just say goodbye?"

He nods and takes the bag.

"All right, just don't bite her," the big woman says.

Cassie runs into my arms and hugs me. "Please don't make me stay with her," she whispers.

"I'm sorry," I whisper back. "Try to get Larry to help you get free."

She squeezes me tighter then. "I love you, Delilah."

"I love you, too, Cassie." I hug her tighter, one last time. "Watch out for yourself."

And then the big, fat lady grabs her out of my grip and slams the door.

Chapter 87

I stare at the closed door. Shut out forever.

I remember when Cassie and I first met, and how everyone who had tried to take care of us had died, and that's why we formed a partnership instead.

And I realize that now I'm somebody. I'm her somebody, living and breathing for a few more hours.

I finally understand why my mom gave her life for me. She didn't do it because it was expected of her, nor did she do it because she was supposed to. She did it because she loved me, and she couldn't bear to see me hurt. She simply *reacted.*

And now I know I have that in me, too. When it mattered, I was able to react and protect someone I loved.

I smile, dig my shamrock necklace out from under my shirt, and kiss it. "Thanks, Mom. I love you."

Then I follow the graveled path back out to the grasslands of Colorado.

#

I don't go far. I walk far enough so I'm sure I'm no longer in the minefield, but the compound is still nearby.

It's pleasant here. The sun's shining, the sky is blue, and there's a warm breeze. I spread out a blanket and have a picnic without any fear of zombies coming along. I put on my sunglasses and lay back in the sun, listening to music. I try to ignore the pain building in my body and killing me slowly.

I enjoy my last moments: the warmth of the sun on my skin, the light wind, the grass soft against my back.

Then I get out my teddy bear and snuggle with it. I fade off to sleep.

#

I wake in the middle of the night and it's very cold. The pain's increased to the worst thing I've ever felt.

Dear God, it feels like my blood is made of fire and my muscles are the coals feeding the flames. I roll back and forth, trying to stop it in some way.

"Please stop, please stop, please stop," I beg the pain, even though I know it won't hear me. I lose track of time, just involved in the virus and trying to make it quit hurting.

"Mommy!" I cry out over and over. I'm hot and then I'm cold. "Mommy!"

But she doesn't come. I hug my bear tighter and eventually, finally, I fall asleep again.

#

I wake up and the sun has risen enough that I can see streaks of pink across the sky.

I sit up and the pain is all gone.

I am zombie.

Chapter 88

I died sometime during the night. I know that now, but I just don't know when it happened.

I hold my arms out in front of me and they're shot through with silver. I take off my shoes and socks and the silver winds up my feet, just under the skin. I run my hands over my face even though I can't see it. I don't feel any cracks.

I had the last batch of The Shot. The last batch, the one that came closest to achieving that evil executive's goal.

Something quickens in my chest, and then slows down.

Did I really die?

I hold my hand against my heart but I don't feel anything. And I was never any good at checking for a pulse.

I don't know. I've definitely changed; the silver showing through my skin proves that.

I think of the girl in the lab, the coldly-smiling girl I now resemble. It hurts to think of it because of Sam, but at some point I think I might want to go back to the base. Talk to her, see what she knows.

I gather up my things and put them all in the backpack. I'm not hungry. I'm not thinking of brains, and I'm not thinking of eating people.

I know I'm different, but I don't know how.

The question is – am I safe to be around?

"Delilah!"

That weird sensation happens in my chest again and I drop my bag. Surely not. Surely I'm hallucinating. She would know better, wouldn't she? She would know better than to come after me.

"Delilah!"

But no, she's there, running toward me with Sunshine by her side.

"Cassie?"

She stops about ten feet away, but I can tell she's been crying. Her hands clench her backpack straps.

"Have you –"

"Changed? Yes." I nod. "Last night. But –"

"Something's different."

"Yes. Cassie, there's something I meant to tell you, about The Shot –"

She holds up her hand, cutting me off. "Are you hungry? Do you feel like eating people?"

"No."

"Good." She drops her bag and runs toward me, even though that's a really stupid thing to do. Cassie, my risk-taker.

I drop to my knees, open my arms and she almost bowls me over with a hug. We're both crying and laughing at the same time.

"Oh, thank God," she says. She hugs me until I choke, then she pulls back. "Wow." She runs her fingertips lightly over my arms, following the silver. "Does it hurt?"

"No." I shake my head. "Cassie, you shouldn't have risked this. You should have stayed in the town, safe."

"I couldn't help it. I had to check. That woman held onto me for hours until they finally made her stop so I could eat dinner. And then I asked if they had a lab and explained about the research. Delilah, they took away my key fob. Said it was too important for a kid."

She's right; her necklace is gone.

"And you were gone, too. And I decided screw it, I didn't want to be around dumb adults anyways."

"What were you going to do if I was a flesh-eating zombie?"

She shrugs. "Didn't happen, so it doesn't matter."

"Cassie." I shake my head again, but it's hard to lecture her when I'm so glad she's here. I take off my USB drive and drape the necklace around her neck.

"You keep this until we get to a lab. Because it *is* important enough for a kid. Look at what the adults did to the world anyways."

She hugs me again, then breaks off to grab her backpack and dab at her eyes. "C'mon, Sunshine."

I pick up a stick and throw it, and Sunshine runs after it with a bark.

"Delilah?"

"Yeah?"

"Thank you for being my somebody."

For a second I think about denying it, shrugging it off, but we both know the truth.

"Glad to," I respond, and take her hand. "C'mon, let's go find that lab and save the world."

Acknowledgments

I originally posted this novel online as a weekly blog. I received help and insights from readers and bloggers, and that input greatly changed the novel. I can't express the amount of gratitude I have for the people who read and commented on that blog. Your insights, kind words and encouragement had a great impact on me and helped me finish the book.

I also want to thank Rocky Mountain Fiction Writers for making this novel a finalist in the Colorado Gold contest (under the title "In A World of Orphans"). They increased my confidence and gave me an opportunity to meet with an agent.

Thank you to the editors at Hot Tree Editing. Their suggestions helped me improved the book and provided some good insights.

Thanks to my friends and parents for the love and support they give me. And thanks to Chris for all of the discussions we had about this story.